BADGE OF THE LAW

BADGE OF THE LAW

Clement Hardin

CHIVERS
THORNDIKE

This Large Print edition is published by BBC Audiobooks Ltd, Bath, England and by Thorndike Press®, Waterville, Maine, USA.

Published in 2004 in the U.K. by arrangement with Golden West Literary Agency.

Published in 2004 in the U.S. by arrangement with Golden West Literary Agency.

U.K. Hardcover ISBN 0–7540–6975–3 (Chivers Large Print)
U.K. Softcover   ISBN 0–7540–6976–1 (Camden Large Print)
U.S. Softcover   ISBN 0–7862–6542–6 (Nightingale)

The text of this Large Print edition is unabridged.
Other aspects of the book may vary from the original edition.

Set in 16 pt. New Times Roman.

Printed in Great Britain on acid-free paper.

British Library Cataloguing in Publication Data available

Library of Congress Cataloging-in-Publication Data

Hardin, Clement, 1916–
   [Badge shooters]
   Badge of the law / by Clement Hardin.
     p. cm.
   Previously published as: The badge shooters.
   ISBN 0–7862–6542–6 (lg. print : sc : alk. paper)
   1. Large type books. I. Title.
PS3527.E9178B33 2004
813'.54—dc22
                                    2004046117

CHAPTER I

Jim Arden thought the barn hostler might have been kicked in the face by one of his own horses. His forehead had a dented look that threw his eyes onto different levels, the left one carrying a drooped lid and a dullness that made it unlikely he could see with it. But there was a real gleam of interest in the other eye as the man peered at Arden, flipping the silver dollar the stranger had passed him.

'Oats,' he mumbled, repeating his instructions. He slapped a flank of the tired, sweat and alkali-smeared buckskin. 'You can leave it to me, mister, I'll take care of him. Must have covered a lot of dry miles today.'

'Rub him down good,' Arden said. 'And go easy on the water. Don't let him drink too much.'

'Sure, sure! I know all about what that desert can do to a good mount. Especially pushed as hard as this one's been!' The good eye settled on Arden again, honed to a shine of pure curiosity. 'Were you heading north? To Gunlock, maybe? Just follow the freight road; you'll find it thirty miles or thereabouts, beyond the hills.'

'I saw a hotel down the street,' Jim Arden remarked, deliberately ignoring the question. 'Can I get a meal there?'

1

The other shook his head. 'Nobody ever did. Try the eat shack yonder.'

It was a crackerbox, standing almost directly opposite the stable. Arden said briefly, 'Thanks,' and walked out through the wide doors, into the street where the last glow of sunset was dying now in bloody ruin.

Lights were already glowing along the double row of buildings set close against a sparsely timbered ridge. Southward, behind him, the desert lay, a flat and gleaming immensity. In the other direction black hills made their low, running, cutout shapes. Thirty miles. Thirty miles to Gunlock.

He frowned thoughtfully, and fading sunset struck across his face and brought out the harder lines and the bleaker planes of it. He was very tired. He could feel the dust that lay in the creases of his skin, could taste its gritty bitterness between his teeth. The shirt was plastered to his body by his own scalding sweat.

Yet there was an habitual wariness in him, even now, that wouldn't relax just because a long day's travel was finished or because a goal lay in sight. He was thinking about the hostler and his questions, the insistent and poorly concealed curiosity of the man.

Arden shrugged, accepting the normal risks of his occupation. Letting food wait for the moment, he turned to walk back in the direction of the hotel. Swiftly, sunset died and left the street in shadow.

A night stage went past him. It quit the town of Sage at a whip-popping run with acrid dust boiling around the wheels, coach lamps bobbing, the horses stretching their necks wildly to the lash. It took a corner at the street's far end with a swoop and was gone into the desert, leaving raised dust that made a kind of yellow fog against the kerosene lantern burning before the hotel. Only a stranger or a damn fool, Arden supposed with a touch of irony, would tackle that desert by day.

He walked through settling dust and entered the hotel.

A bell jangled as he kicked the door shut. The empty lobby had the very smell of dust. An old man in carpet slippers came shuffling through a door behind the desk, to lay the register open and stand waiting as Arden walked over and took the pen from a saucer filled with lead shot.

'Staying long?'

'Just tonight,' said Arden. He hesitated, debating a signature, nearly convinced his real name would be safe enough to use here. But with a shrug he decided otherwise and wrote 'James Bard' instead, and after it, 'Santa Fe.'

'Your first time in our city, Mr. Bard?'

'I don't know this end of the Territory at all,' he admitted briefly, as he took the key the old man handed him.

'Well, there's Gunlock, just beyond them

hills you may have seen on the north,' the hotel man suggested. 'Cattle country, in there. Gunlock folks keep pretty much to themselves, you know.'

'Is that a fact?' grunted Jim Arden. This could get monotonous—the repeated questions, the open curiosity. They kept shoving this Gunlock Valley at him, but he was not ready yet to take the bait. He merely laid a silver dollar on the desk and turned toward the curtained archway that opened on a narrow corridor lined with rooms.

'That'll be number five, Mr. Bard,' the man called after him. 'Guess you can find it all right.'

He found it—though there was little enough, besides the numbers painted on the doors, to distinguish these crude, cheaply furnished cubicles one from another. Arden took off his hat and tossed it on the sagging bed, ran his fingers through hair that was stiff with dirt and sweat. The room held a commode with a spotted mirror, a wash basin and pitcher. Checking first to be sure the pitcher held water, Arden proceeded to strip to the waist, revealing a lean, hard torso that carried no spare weight. It was shades lighter than the sun-darkened skin of the face and throat above it. He filled the basin and sluiced himself, ducked his head, toweled vigorously. He felt better thereafter, some of the tiredness seeming to wash away with the sweat and grime.

He had his razor in his pocket. Inspection in the mirror, however, decided him that the beard shadowing his sloping jaws could be allowed to go a little longer. So he ran a comb through dripping hair, laying it long and flat above his ears, and got back into the shirt he'd removed. As he slipped the tails into his pants and buckled them up, the badge he wore pinned to the underside of the wide leather belt caught light from the ceiling lamp; he paused a moment, looking at it.

How long was it, now, that he'd carried the badge and the gun for the United States Marshal's Office? Jim Arden totted it up and was surprised. Seven years—as long as that. And before, there'd been the Army. Yes, he guessed he was the government's man, all right.

A machine, a girl had called him once. A machine without heart or blood or will, meant only for duty and carrying a gun and killing on command; whether for a sergeant's chevrons on his tunic or a marshal's badge pinned to his belt. It was so long ago the girl said it that Jim Arden had forgotten her name, had all but forgotten her face; yet he knew the memory of the words was still with him in the set of the mouth, in the shadows of the eyes that looked back at him from the mirror on the dingy wall.

He studied that face, another thought suddenly returning. That fellow McQueen, who'd broken under pressure yesterday and come through with the information he needed to send him north across the desert—what was it McQueen seemed to read in his tormentor's eyes, in that last moment before he quailed and began his wild talking? Could it really be there was a devil in him somewhere? Something in-human, that the years of following the badge and the gun had put there?

Arden shook his head impatiently, and shoved the buckle's hasp into the proper hole. A record as good as his cost something; there was no point, he told himself, in taking seriously the self-doubts that came to a man in his moments of weariness. Remember, instead, the job he had to do here, the job that had caused him to be sent into this section of New Mexico Territory. Others in the marshal's office had tried their best at it and failed.

When you served the law, you set yourself apart. You were a dedicated man, or you were nothing.

Deliberately Arden turned for the shell belt and holster he'd draped across the bed post and fitted them into place, the gun with its hand-rubbed walnut grips set just so against his leg. He picked up his hat, blew the lamp and stepped once more into the corridor.

A man stood before the lobby desk, the registry book open and a finger resting on the page. His head snapped up as Arden appeared in the arch. Their looks met and held for a long second; the lawman saw a tall man, taller by a little than himself, and the belligerent thrust of an unusually long jaw. Coal black eyes seemed to stab at him. Neither spoke; the look was all that passed between them. Arden went on, across the cheap carpet and into gathered dusk. The bell jangled again as he pulled the door to behind him. But then he did pause, for a long moment, with his hand still on the knob.

Now who would be taking such an interest in a signature in the register?

At once, caution was a taut, steel thread strung all through him. A roused instinct for danger sharpened his senses. As he came down the broad steps to the level of the street and then swung north, the pound of his own heels on the board walk seemed to him a monstrous sound, that echoed off the silent faces of encroaching building fronts.

He walked without haste, but as he went he probed the shadows and listened for sound at his back. The street, in this first hour of full darkness, lay empty and without light except where an occasional window or door spilled yellow lamp glow across sidewalk and dust. North of town, hills cut their black line across the lower reaches of the sky.

On the opposite side of the street, now, he could see the plate glass of the eat shack. He saw something more: a man waited at the corner of the small square building. No, there were two! They stood quite motionless, but he could see them outlined against the window. And, remembering his words with the stable hostler, Arden had a sudden, instinctive knowledge that they were waiting for him.

At once he halted, and side-stepped to place himself in the deeper shadow between buildings at his left. The reaction to his disappearance was immediate. Against the window glow, he saw that pair break from their position at the eat shack corner. An unintelligible word or two drifted across the stillness. One of the men halted uncertainly, silhouetted as he stared in Arden's direction; the other crossed the planking and at once began circling into the empty street.

Jim Arden's right hand dipped and the butt of the belt gun settled into his palm; he brought the weapon out, held close against his hip and leveled. *If it was me,* he thought, *I'd have a stakeout in the barn, just in case!* If he added the lantern-jawed man from the hotel lobby, he'd be willing to place the odds at a probable four to one. *Always shade it a little in favor of the other side . . .*

So far there'd been no sound from the direction of the hotel; Arden didn't like the thought of someone moving in behind him. He pulled back into the slot between the buildings. As he did, some glimpse of his movement, some glimmer of reflected light from gun barrel, must have reached the watching man across the street, because there was a sudden cry from over there that sounded like a name: 'Daugherty!' But this was lost in Arden's own footsteps as he turned abruptly and headed away from the street, one sleeve brushing the dark wall.

Behind the buildings lay open ground, and the near lift of the long ridge that basked the town. Arden rounded the corner and swung north again. In so doing his boot made contact with a discarded bucket and it was sent flying, to bounce and rattle.

At once, to his rear, a gun let loose—a single roar of sound, a stabbing bullet.

Arden halted, whipping about as he jammed himself back against the rough wall. So that was how they wanted to play the hand! His gun leaped, but he dropped the muzzle again. He had no target, and to shoot would merely make one of himself. He had no intention of letting Daugherty—the man from the hotel— get in another shot. He turned and went on, running lightly now.

Just ahead he saw faintly the loom of the livery's rear end, and then a black pattern of corral poles. He reached this and laid a hand on a tooth-gnawed pole while he listened. It seemed to him the night was suddenly alive with running men. Daugherty was coming up from behind. To his right, from the direction of the street, someone else was hurrying

9

toward him along the near side of the barn. That would be one of the pair he'd seen at the eat shack window.

He slipped between the bars with a single easy movement, straightening and setting off quickly across the hoof-churned corral. He had almost reached the yonder side when, unmistakably, he heard still another runner approaching from dead ahead, having circled the barn on the north.

So they had him on three sides, now.

The odds were too great for anyone to stand and let them close in like this. Still, there was an alternative. A door of the livery opened onto this corral in which they had him trapped; it traveled on an overhead track, and a thin strip of blackness showed it was open wide enough for him to slip through. Without hesitation he crossed to this door, while the pound of boots thudded nearer.

About to slip inside, he remembered his first hunch—that yet a fourth member of the gang might be waiting inside the barn to prevent him getting to his horse once they closed the bag on him. This made him take the opening at a swift, plunging dive. He went to hands and knees on slick straw and splintered boards, well within the thick inner darkness. And there he crouched, listening and smelling the familiar odors of horses and hay and mice.

It was as though all sound had stopped. The walls muffled any movement outside, and around him there was only a booming, musty silence. In a stall, up forward, a horse blew through its nostrils and a hoof struck a timber. That was all.

At the front of the building, gaping doors framed the houses across the street with their yellow windows and, above the jagged profile of roofs and false fronts, a strip of pale sky. It made the blackness within the barn all the more complete. Eyes probing, Arden lifted his gun and his left hand brushed a wisp of loose straw from the barrel.

He was rising to his feet when the low voice spoke, somewhere startlingly near, and caused him to freeze.

'I'd be damned careful there—*lawman!*'

CHAPTER II

Breath clogged briefly in Arden's throat and then began again, shallowly. For a long moment he stayed where he was, at a crouch, his knees just lifted off the floor, the fingers of his left hand bracing him and ready to push him upward. And the voice said, 'There's just the two of us. My boys have got this barn wrapped up and nobody's going to interfere with them. So don't make any mistakes!'

It seemed impossible to place the location of the voice—the half-whispered words chased each other through the barn, muffled by bales of hay and close partitions, echoing from the high roof. Yet Arden felt that the speaker must be somewhere very close; and when a revolver's hammer drew back to cock, the sound was startlingly clear.

That made him move. He flung himself sideward. His left hand felt the shape of a squared bale of hay and he went over it, to drop behind what protection it could give.

A low chuckle followed him. 'That's right. Hunt cover! I'm behind a pretty stout partition, here. Gunplay's not going to get us anything.'

Sprawled with his head pulled down and both elbows on the floor, Arden said, 'What is it you want, then?'

12

'A couple of words with you.'

It was a long moment before he answered. 'All right—Frank Trace. If you have anything worth saying, I suppose I'll listen.'

The voice came, husky with surprise, 'What was that name you called me?'

'You heard, I think. Why can't we lay this thing out, cold turkey?'

Again a pause. 'Suits me, Arden,' the voice said finally. 'Life's short enough without beating around bushes. But do you mind telling me how you knew who I was?'

'Couldn't have been anybody else, not this close to Gunlock. But me, I'm a stranger here. It puzzles me how that barnman could have recognized me.'

'He didn't. He just figured you for a lawman—the way you came out of the desert.'

'But you called my name.'

'That's right. I did.'

Arden was getting cramped. He shifted position slightly and straw slithered under him. He thought now he had his man placed somewhere in front of him and to the right. He laid his gun barrel across the edge of the hay bale, rested it there as he tried to line up the source of the voice.

Still no sound from outside. Probably the people of Sage were staying well away from whatever was going on here. Beyond the big front entrance of the stable a rider passed unhurriedly along the street; the clop of hoofs

13

quickly died, muffled in thick dust.

When the voice came again, it was lifted to a conversational level. 'Don't tell me you're surprised I'd know you by reputation, Jim Arden. You've got a pretty good one.'

'Thanks,' the lawman answered dryly.

'So it seemed it might be a good thing if we could have a friendly talk.'

'When somebody threw a bullet at me, I didn't get the idea it was a talk I was wanted for!'

Frank Trace hesitated. 'I'm sorry about that,' he said, seriously. 'Really sorry. The boys were edgy. The idea wasn't to hurt you.'

'Oh, it wasn't?'

'We only wanted to find out what you were up to. This is sort of an isolated section, you know, but news leaks in. When we heard Jim Arden had been sighted heading this way, asking questions about us, we were naturally concerned.'

'Naturally.' Arden was thinking fast. Could it have been McQueen who passed the word? No, not necessarily. It might have been any of a dozen others. You never knew, even when you asked the most guarded questions, what enemy you might be tipping your hand to.

He said, 'It's the first time you and your gang have had federal law on your heels. The whole Southwest knows about your setup in Gunlock, how you and that political machine you work for have got local law tied up, have

14

even got wires into the right places in Santa Fe. You lead your gang wherever you feel like, pull any kind of job you want, and then you fade back behind the hills and you know no one can touch you.

'But you made your slip when you murdered that Army paymaster down by Lordsburg. Even your boss can't help you out of that one. Because Merl Riling himself won't buy the federal marshal's office!'

He waited for an answer. It was a long time coming; when the man spoke again, it was on a note of hurt innocence.

'Arden! I swear I don't know what you're getting at, talking about a machine! The law hasn't got a thing on me or my boys. Oh, I know there's been loose talk. Some people, I guess, can't help envying a free-ranging bunch like us. Sure we move around a lot, trade in livestock, pick up a few horses here and there.'

'Just how do you mean, "pick them up"?'

Frank Trace swore. 'Man, I'm trying to convince you we're legitimate! And we don't know a single damn thing about that Lordsburg job.'

'Then what's got you worried? Why was your man so quick to hit a trigger?'

That seemed to have stopped the other for an instant. 'All right,' Trace said at last. 'Maybe a few little jobs have been laid to us. Nothing big. We certainly don't want trouble with the federal government—or anyone who carries your record.'

'That's too bad,' Arden said shortly. 'Because I'm afraid you've got it!'

'Now, hold on. I heard tell that the ones who killed the paymaster wore masks. You've got no way to tie it to us.'

'Not yet, maybe, not directly. But I've got a witness that places you close to the scene, at about the right time. That should do for a start. It's more than we ever had.'

'A witness? Who would dare—' Trace suddenly broke off in midsentence.

'Yes?' Arden prompted him. 'What were you about to say?'

The outlaw knew he'd almost made a mistake. He back-tracked and tried again.

'Whoever it is, he's lying! We'll produce witnesses of our own, who can prove we were in Gunlock.'

'If you can do that, you're in luck. I'll have to check it out.'

'And you really figure to come ahead?' the other demanded, tightly. 'Listen to me, Arden! Gunlock's my territory. I got friends in there. They won't like an outsider nosing around asking questions, making accusations against my boys and me. They won't like it at all.'

'You sure there might not be another side to that picture? Maybe you're afraid a few people in Gunlock might have nerve enough to talk, if a federal man could once reach them. It just might be the machine hasn't got as strong a

16

hold as it looks from outside. And in that case, just maybe I can break it.'

'Alone?' He heard, in the stillness, the other's long-drawn breath. 'Arden,' Frank Trace said finally, 'I like a man with guts. From what I've heard, I got a hunch I could have liked you—if you didn't insist on putting us on opposite sides of the fence this way.

'But if that's your choosing, then come ahead! Come by yourself, or with an army. I won't guarantee what you may run into.'

'I don't expect any guarantees! But I can tell you now, I'll be alone; the marshal's office hasn't got any more men than it needs, spread thin over a territory this size. So there's no need for you to hold back if you want trouble. Go ahead and whistle up your dogs, and we can have it out right now. Four against one.'

He heard Frank Trace swear, a single tearing oath. The stillness piled up, during a long ticking of silent seconds. Then, 'I said before, Arden—I like a man with guts!'

There was a slithering sound in the straw beyond that partition, as a body changed position. Jim Arden half straightened and his gun leveled and ground hard against his fingers. The small, whispering noises ran out and then as suddenly ceased though he waited, listening, until the muscles of his crouching body began once more to cramp and knot. The sound of his own breathing was all he heard now, except for an occasional snuffle

17

and stomp of a horse. Slowly, the feeling descended on him that he was alone.

He spoke the outlaw's name and got no answer. Conviction grew to a certainty; Arden eased to his feet and, still carrying the ready gun, groped his way forward. His fingers touched rough wood of the partition behind which Frank Trace had crouched to carry on his talk. The blackness of the wall beyond was broken by the lighter gray of a side door standing partly open on the night. A small breeze sucked through it, fanning against his face.

He lowered his gun, slowly, knowing now that the man was gone. He shoved the weapon into its holster and stood with his hand resting on it, as he listened to the muffled silence of the barn and such few sounds as came on the desert-dry wind.

So that was that. A challenge had been given and accepted; the gage was laid down. The next move in this deadly game rode with him.

CHAPTER III

Standing there he tried to build a mental image to fit the voice that had come out of the piled shadows. It had been a young man's voice, with a pleasing timbre and very little of the crudeness of an illiterate tough. Nothing he'd heard of this Frank Trace tended to make him think the man would be anything other than a dangerous enemy.

A frown tightened the edges of his mouth and Jim Arden felt uneasiness begin to work inside his empty belly. It was too quiet. He could hear no sound of the ones who'd had this barn surrounded, a moment ago; but did that mean they had left? It could be they only wanted him to think so, and were waiting for him to walk out through those wide forward doors so they could cut him down.

Would they dare? This wasn't Gunlock. Would they turn their guns on a federal marshal, here in neutral territory?

He raised a hand, ran the flat of his thumb along the stubbled line of his jaw and felt the faint sweat that had gathered there. And then Jim Arden dropped his arm, and his shoulders settled as he made his decision.

He went forward to the stall where he had seen the hostler place his buckskin gelding, and the bronc lifted its head from the manger and looked around at him. 'Sorry, fellow,' Arden said, as he moved to fetch his saddle and gear from the nail where they had been hung.

The blanket was still sweat-soaked, and he spread out the wrinkles with particular care, working by feel and such dim light as reached him from the street doors. The buckskin resented being put under the saddle again, and swelled its barrel when Arden was cinching up; a knee in the ribs stopped that maneuver. At least, he thought, the horse had had a graining. Its owner would have to pull his belt tighter than the cinch, on the supper he apparently wasn't going to get. He forced the bit in place, then went to get his blanket roll from the shelf where he'd thrown it, earlier, after digging out his razor.

His groping fingers told him at once that someone else had unlashed the roll and gone through it. Jim Arden swore a little, under his breath. This, undoubtedly, was how they'd found the means of knowing who he was. Working as quickly as he could, he reassembled the roll and slung it behind the saddle and lashed it down. Afterward, he led the bronc out into the center aisle, and stood with the reins in his hand, debating.

There were two ways to go—front or rear. He considered them both and decided that if anyone was waiting for him it would most likely be with the expectation that he was going to walk out through the wide main doors, heading for the eat shack across the street. Already he'd delayed so long they might be growing suspicious.

So he led his horse instead back along the aisle to the rear door that opened onto the night corral. It creaked a little as he pushed it open all the way.

The night was lighter than he had expected, and he realized that over eastward the moon must be edging above the horizon. He saw the pattern of the corral poles and noticed that all but one bar of the gate was down. The hill behind the town lifted toward a long, running crest studded with scrub cedar, and Venus shone all alone in a deepening sky. Nothing moved, anywhere.

He stepped into the saddle, the leather making slight popping noises; he drew his gun. Then, with a quick jab of heels, Arden kicked the buckskin and it exploded forward as he ducked his head to clear the doorway.

By the time he had straightened, they were half way across the corral. Two more strides brought them to the gate, and the buckskin took the one low bar with a clean leap and hit the ground beyond, running. At the same moment something moved at the edge of Arden's vision. He twisted around, swinging the Colt, as a gun roared and split the dark.

A bullet winged close, within inches. His own thumb slipped off the hammer-spur and his sixgun smashed a wild shot as the buckskin ran ahead. He heard a voice shout exultantly, *'I got him!'*

Jim Arden said between his teeth, 'The hell you have!'

He groped for his holster and shoved his own gun home. It wouldn't help him now.

There was yelling and confusion, raised by the gunfire, but this all lay behind him. The earth was lifting as the buckskin hit the base of the long ridge. When the animal tried to swerve aside and run with the contour of the ground, Arden pulled its head back and set it straight at the rise, instead. The gelding arched its neck in protest, but it yielded to the bit and they started up.

Scrub growth scratched against stirrup fenders and, as this rise steepened, the buckskin began having trouble in loose soil. When a straight climb became no longer possible, Arden pulled in and let the bronc take the rest of the distance at its own pace, quartering up the last steep pitch and laboring over it. At the top, he paused for a look behind him.

The town lay back there, along the foot of the ridge—a shapeless pattern of wooden buildings picked out in squares of yellow window light. Beyond, desert stretched flat as a table, and now a huge white moon stood clear of the horizon and stained the alkali wastes with silver. By its light, Jim Arden saw the horsemen who suddenly broke out of shadows at the rear of the big barn and came running straight at the hill. He counted three riders and didn't wait for more, but turned instead and kicked his horse on across the flat crest of the ridge and down the farther slope.

This was a long, slanting hogback, with another rise beyond. Arden took the dip and the second climb, pushing his horse as fast as he dared across treacherous ground. Behind him a single shot cracked the night's stillness; the sound pulled Arden's mouth down, hard. Someone back there was shooting at shadows. Trace's men had no intention of letting the lawman go, after they'd once had him cornered.

Arden kicked more speed out of the gelding. He knew he was still well in front, running alone in the night with the hammering of his own bronc's hoofs.

He put two more ridges behind him and a little later came upon an open stretch that had been scarred by a half dozen twisting arroyos. The ground tilted slightly to the north, where it was bordered by tangled growth and by an outriding spur of the hills. Jim Arden dropped over the lip of one of the shallow cuts and pointed in the direction of the brush.

He knew, though, that the buckskin had already given more than it should, tired as it was to begin with. Its stride was beginning to falter; and by the time the chaparral loomed just ahead, with the moon glinting from a thousand spiky branches, it was plain they could run no farther. He spoke encouragement to his horse, and its legs trembled with the final surge that lifted them out of the arroyo and into the thorny arms. Immediately Jim Arden reined in, and swung swiftly down from the saddle.

Holding the reins, he drew his gun and carefully parted the branches. He didn't have to wait long—a couple of minutes, perhaps—before a pound of hoofs began to make itself heard in the early night. Riders came into view there at the far end of the open. As they came on, weaving a black pattern, he counted six: a couple more than he had been figuring. The moonlight was bright enough that he should have been able to pick one or two of them out of their saddles, but this wasn't what he had in mind.

With the horses drawing nearer he reached and got a hold on the buckskin's headstall, but the precaution wasn't needed. Now one of the horsemen raised a shout and Arden thought for a moment he'd been discovered. But the leader—he guessed it must be Frank Trace himself—was only calling his men together before they plunged into the brush. Arden watched them confer, while their horses stomped and milled restlessly.

Then the whole half dozen were pouring up into the chaparral at a point some hundred yards distant from where he stood. The crashing of their horses through brush grew gradually fainter; now and then the voices of the men sounded, calling back and forth. Then all sound died and silence fell upon the night.

With a long drag of breath, Arden let the tension ease out of him.

No man liked being forced to run for his life. Still, it had been only the first hand in this game. He'd known he could expect trouble once he rode into Gunlock; but the hornet's nest he'd stirred up tonight, in a town thirty miles away, had come as a complete surprise. It had never occurred to him that word of his activities in the Lordsburg case might precede him north, or alarm Tracy badly enough to bring the outlaw out of his Gunlock Valley hole-in-the-wall in an attempt to head him off. Perhaps Trace had already thought he could put the law off his trail with words—and with a bullet if the words failed. In any event, he was in real trouble and apparently he knew it.

And in the next round, Jim Arden meant to hold some of the high cards.

Deliberately, he punched the spent shells from his Colt and reloaded, dropped the gun back into its holster. Thirty miles to Gunlock, he thought. Another man might have been inclinded to second thoughts about the challenge he'd taken, there in the musty darkness of the barn, but not Jim Arden. Like a machine set to do a job, he was already casting ahead, computing his chances. Getting into Gunlock was the problem. Trace's men would stop him if they could; but there might be a few hours, while they were searching this rough country near Sage, when the road would be open.

Accordingly, Jim Arden turned once more to his tired buckskin. He checked the cinches, and lifted himself into the saddle.

CHAPTER IV

The freight road climbed to a long and shallow pass before it started down again. This was the actual gateway to the valley. Pine stood scattered over the shouldering humps, and northward another range of hills, blue with distance, marked Gunlock's far rim.

Wood smoke tanging thin air gave Arden a few moments' warning before he caught sight of the buildings that clustered against a face of rock, where the pass narrowed. He pulled in, narrowly studying them. There was one structure of two stories, with a balcony over the long porch. There was a log barn and sheds and a corral, all the timbers weathered to a neutral gray by the storms that must hit this pass. He saw a canvas-hooded freight rig and trailer, the teams unhooked; the freighter was moving about the mules adjusting feed bags while a swamper greased one of the big wheels.

The sun, standing high overhead, told Arden it was well toward noon. His empty belly told him that except for a single stringy jack, knocked over just at sunrise that morning, he'd eaten nothing much in near thirty hours. Moreover, he'd traveled through most of the night, only holing up for a couple of hours after his scanty pre-dawn meal. He was fine-strung, edgey with exhaustion. It put him in an impatient mood as he sat looking this place over and trying to come to a decision about it.

The sound of an ax chopping firewood drifted across the stillness. One of the mules in the wagon teams loosed a bray that shivered echoes from the overhanging face of rock behind the roadhouse. Smoke stood in a straight pencil line above the rock-and-daub chimney. That meant a stove fire, food cooking.

Arden shifted in saddle, frowning. This might be no more than what it looked to be, a way station for the freight outfits that made the haul across to Gunlock, and for a stageline if one used this route. But it didn't feel right to Jim Arden. Then he heard the jangle of a screen door slamming, and he saw the man who walked out onto the porch and stood with sunlight slanting against him, and picking out a glint of brass from a low-slung cartridge belt at his waist. His face was in shadow but the stranger knew this man was studying him, with a fine attention.

Arden nudged the tired horse forward.

He rode unhurriedly, letting his body give to the buckskin's jogging. The ax had stilled, he realized, and the thud of hoofs into trail dust laid the only sound across the afternoon. The man on the porch stood unmoving and watched him come. Three hundred yards

28

farther on, this road was swallowed by pine and by the encroaching walls of the pass; Arden downed a temptation to sink spurs and strike for timber.

He couldn't outrun a bullet.

As he neared the wagons, the swamper glanced up from the wheel he'd been greasing, then straightened and stood with the cloth-wrapped stick in one hand and the bucket of daub in the other. He was a bucktoothed kid, with a look of no great intelligence. He nodded greeting and said, 'Howdy.'

Arden drew rein. Aware that what he said carried to the listening ears of the man on the porch, he asked casually, 'What place is this?'

'Pete Hawks'.'

'Can I get a meal here?'

'That, among other things.' And the kid snickered a little, and jerked his head toward a couple of posts where a row of garments fluttered from a clothesline. Arden hadn't noticed them before; they were women's garments—intimate and tawdry, hanging there in the open light of day.

So that was the kind of place it was!

He rode on, without hurry, straight toward the roadhouse where the man he had picked to be Pete Hawks stood half in sun and half in shadow, teetering on broad bootsoles at the edge of the steps. He was a solid figure of a man, with heavy brows and a mouth half hidden by an untrimmed brush of black mustache. He looked at the rider and at the horse, and as Arden halted he said heavily, 'You lookin' for grub, are you? It's an off hour, but I reckon I could fix you up.'

'Good enough,' said Arden. 'What's on the menu?'

'Anything you like, so long as it's beef and beans.'

'Beef and beans sounds fine,' said Arden, and watched the man heel around and walk into the building. He hesitated just a moment. He thought he could almost feel the pressure of other, watching eyes; and he could only guess at what a suspicious move might get him. But he needed that meal.

So he dropped reins and stepped down, moving slowly and casually. He gave the hull a shake to ease the set of it, lifted the buckskin's nigh rear leg to inspect the hoof, and then went up the steps and across the porch, and pulled open the screen.

He entered a large low room that contained, chiefly, a number of tables, and at one side a counter with a stairway beyond it, running up to rooms on the second floor. There was another door that his nose told him must lead to the kitchen. At one of the rear tables, a couple of women looked up from their coffee cups. They were a frowzy pair, one of them in a soiled wrapper, and both wearing the wreckage of last night's make-up. Arden thought he could smell their cheap perfume clear across the length of the room.

They stared with a frank and hostile curiosity at the stranger; so did the man who stood in front of the counter with an elbow leaning on the wood, and a dice box in his hands.

He had close-cropped red hair, and one cheek carried the shine of scar tissue where the flesh might have been mauled in a fight. Dice clicked in the cup as he rocked it idly between his palms, and he said, 'Heading for Gunlock?'

Arden considered the man for a long moment before he answered, noting the thrust of a holstered gun against his hip, the cold quality of his stare. 'I'm told that's where this road goes.'

The answer didn't seem to please the man. 'You got business?'

'Yes,' said Arden curtly. 'My own!'

It was no way to ease suspicions, but the questions roweled him and turned him reckless. If there had to be trouble, then let it come! He heard a muffled sound from one of the women, but he didn't take his waiting look from the man at the bar. He saw something happen to the man's face—like a bunching of the muscles under the hard, smooth-shaven cheeks. Slowly, the man's hand reached around and set the dice cup on the counter while his eyes held hard on Arden's.

Then Pete Hawks was coming back from the

kitchen, moving briskly, showing his teeth in a grin beneath the heavy black mustache. Either he didn't sense the tension that stretched tautly here, or he chose to ignore it. He told Arden, 'Your food will be ready in a couple of shakes. Have a drink, while you're waiting.'

An instant, Arden hesitated while his look still measured the redhead. Then he shrugged. 'Why not?' Hawks had already moved around a corner of the bar and was bringing up a bottle and glasses. He poured a drink for himself and for the stranger, queried the third man with a look which the latter answered by a curt shake of the head. The redhead moved aside as Arden stepped over and took his glass. His eyes held on the stranger. There was still danger in him.

Outside, the sound of the chopping ax resumed, in the warm noontime stillness.

Hawks tossed off his own drink, wiped his mustache on the ball of a thumb. 'Heading for Gunlock?' he asked, with the same forced casualness with which everyone asked that question.

The redhead said dryly, before the stranger could have answered, 'He don't want to talk about himself, Pete.'

The grin only widened. 'Oh, sure he does! I'm Pete Hawks,' he went on pleasantly. 'This here is Tab Slagoe. You got a name, maybe?'

Arden merely raised his glass to his lips, not speaking. When he lowered it, half empty, he

32

saw the redhead poised in a half crouch. Slagoe's face had taken on angry color, and the scar on his left cheek stood out whitely. He said, 'Do you *want* trouble, mister?'

'Now, Tab,' said Hawks with a look of mild reproof. He spread his big hands flat on the counter, and turned his attention again to the stranger. 'Maybe you don't quite understand how it is. Gunlock is a sort of shut-in place; not many strangers come in. Them that do—well, it's a long distance from here to a county seat, and if we weren't careful there's no telling what sort might be moving in and taking over. So, Gunlock folks kind of expect me to watch the road, screen out the undesirables, if you know what I mean.

'Nothing personal,' he added, quickly, in the same bland tone. 'I'm sure you understand that. Still, I'm going to have to ask you right out. What's your business in Gunlock? Think it over careful, and give us a straight answer!'

There was no answering smile in Jim Arden's eyes. 'And suppose I don't?'

Pete Hawks' toothy smile seemed to congeal on his face. The heavy mustache drooped; the eyes narrowed a trifle. Slowly he straightened, his hands falling to his sides. 'You don't really mean that!'

An old woman stuck her head in through the kitchen door. 'Grub's ready,' she announced into the sudden, collected silence.

'Just hold it,' Hawks ordered, without

looking at her, and she withdrew.

'We're waiting,' Tab Slagoe remarked in a voice that was honed almost to a whisper.

Jim Arden looked from one to the other of this pair. He saw that the redhead's right fist had pulled back, to hang a spare inch from the butt of his holstered gun. Because of the counter, he couldn't even see what Pete Hawks might be doing—perhaps already palming a bar weapon. He took a slow breath and let his shoulders settle, the way he unconsciouly did before he went for his gun. 'All right,' he began, harshly. 'Any time you want to start it!'

And then he was interrupted as someone came running up the steps and across the porch, and burst into the room.

CHAPTER V

Arden made a hasty, sideward movement that swung him around so he could face the newcomer, without letting either of the men at the counter out of his line of vision; his hand was already grabbing at his gun but he let it rest in holster, seeing that no other weapon was being cleared.

It was a woman who stood in the doorway, one hand still holding the screen open. No, a girl—dressed in blue jeans and half boots, and a blouse that showed quite plainly the youthful shape of her. A wide-brimmed hat was held in place by a whang strap, below a stubborn chin. The pallor of her cheeks told Arden that she was frightened, or angry. More probably both.

Her full breast lifted. 'Hawks!' the girl cried hoarsely. 'Where have you got her?'

'Why, now,' Pete Hawks exclaimed. 'Who would you be talking about, Miss Clevenger?'

'You know very well who!' she retorted. 'My sister.'

Hawks spread empty hands. 'What would have give you the notion she might be here, Nan?'

'Take a look outside,' she snapped, and gestured impatiently through the door. For the first time, now, Arden noticed the pair of horses that had joined his own buckskin, below the porch railing. 'The black is Dulcie's—and don't tell me you didn't know it! He was in your shed; the saddle, too. Besides, there's this.' She was digging into a pocket of her blouse, bringing out a fold of paper which she flung down contemptuously. 'Frank Trace had the gall to send Dulcie a note, telling her to meet him in this—this *dive* of yours.'

Arden shot a glance at Hawks and surprised the look of consternation that had cut through the man's habitual smiling mask. There were undercurrents here, he thought. Tab Slagoe's scarred face showed puzzlement. With all their eyes watching him, Pete Hawks lifted a hand and rubbed it across his forehead, as he hunted an answer. But then he shook his head, and the smile was back again. 'I'm telling you, Nan,' he said, 'you're mistaken.'

'And *you're* a damn poor liar!' she retorted, with a spirit that Arden instantly liked.

He watched as she flung her glance about the room, letting it rest for a contemptuous moment on the pair of Hawks' girls. Then her eye lit on the door of the kitchen, yonder; resolution firmed her jaw and she started for there, heading straight across the room.

Tab Slagoe made a move as though to intercept her but dropped his hand. In a dead silence, broken only by the tap of the girl's riding boots and the distant chopping of the ax, Nan Clevenger went to that door and walked through it, and a moment later her voice came back as she hurled questions at the cook. But now Arden was watching Tab Slagoe, seeing his glance turn to the note she had flung down. He heard Pete Hawks suck in an involuntary breath as the redhead took a step and leaned to pick the paper up. Slagoe unfolded it and glanced at the writing. Slowly a scowl built upon his face. He lifted his head, and his eyes sought Pete Hawks.

'How much do you know about his?' he demanded harshly.

Looking at Hawks, Arden thought he read sudden fear in the man. 'How would I know what Frank Trace might have wrote to some female?' Hawks was almost stammering. Then he broke off as Nan Clevenger came back from her unrewarded search of the kitchen.

Less certain now, she again stood and let her look range the place; and now, apparently, she discovered the stairway to the second floor. Arden saw her head lift, saw her eyes darken with the thought that struck her.

'You haven't put her up *there*?' she cried, and her voice held shock. 'You wouldn't! Even Frank Trace would have more respect for a girl.'

Next moment she was running toward the stairs. It was Hawks himself who moved quickly from behind his counter, to head her off before she could reach them. She turned and swung a fist that struck him on the side of the head. 'Get away from me!' she cried.

The blow had surprised him but likely not hurt him much, though it coarsened his voice with anger. 'There's nothin' up there for you to see!' he grunted. 'Don't be a fool.' His big paw closed on her arm, trapping it, and he tried to swing her away from the steps.

'Let me go!' Nan Clevenger gasped, and fought to pull free. She struck at him again, and the splat of her knuckles against the big man's cheek mingled with his grunt of pain and anger.

Jim Arden said, 'Let go of her, Hawks.'

For that moment they'd all of them—even the suspicious Tab Slagoe—forgotten the man from across the pass. It gave him time to slip his gun and lay the muzzle of it squarely on Pete Hawks' thick middle.

Over at the other end of the room, one of the women toppled her chair as she leaped to her feet with a choked scream. 'Pete! *Watch it!*' Slowly the man turned his head. Tab Slagoe had started a move toward his own holster, but a warning glance from Arden made him check it. For a moment the scene held, frozen by the menace of the Colt.

Then Slagoe found his tongue. The scar on his battered cheek gleamed as he said, tightly, 'You better not make any mistake, Arden. This is none of your mix!'

Arden!

They'd had him pegged all along. The name seemed to have slipped from Slagoe's tongue unnoticed, and the lawman let it go by him the same way. He said coldly, 'Don't make any mistake, yourself. Turn around and let's see you lay your hands on the bar!' And when this had been done, he said with grudging submission, 'Now you, Hawks. Stand away from the girl.'

Hawks' face had a look of bloated, congested fury; the mark of Nan Clevenger's fist showed plain against it. He took his hand off the girl and let it drop to his side, but he said, 'She's got no business goin' up those steps. Damn it, I've told her already that her sister ain't—'

She wasn't even listening. She was staring past him, and now Hawks broke off and turned to see the person who stood at the head of the stairwell, with one hand upon the railing and the other pressed against her breast.

Arden would have known at once the two girls were sisters. There was a clear family resemblance, though Dulcie Clevenger looked at first glance a little softer, a little more feminine, perhaps without some of Nan's capable strength. But that might have been due in part to the way she stood there, and the shocked dread she showed at her discovery. In part, too, to the fact that she was dressed in a full, soft skirt and frilly bodice, by contrast to her older sister's blouse and jeans.

Now, as Nan came resolutely up the steps, Dulcie drew back from what she saw in her face. 'How'd you find me?' she gasped. 'You had no right to follow me here! Can't you leave me alone?'

'Where are your things?' her sister demanded. 'You're leaving.'

'No!'

Without arguing, Nan brushed by her; she must have seen the door her sister had left standing open. Dulcie cried a protest but only stood there, miserable, gnawing at her lip. And Jim Arden turned his attention back to the pair he held under his gun.

'You, Hawks,' he said. 'I don't trust you. Come over here with Slagoe and put your hands on the bar, where I can see them.'

The big man shot him a glowering look, then shrugged and moved to obey the order. Arden shot a glance at Hawks' girls, who were watching all this in narrow-eyed silence. Tab Slagoe said heavily, 'You didn't deny that your name is Arden!'

The lawman studied him with an expression that revealed nothing. 'Why should I bother denying anything, to you?'

'Whoever you are,' Pete Hawks grunted, showing Arden a face that held a faint beading of sweat, under pressure of the cocked and pointed gun, 'I wouldn't want to be the man to come between Frank Trace and a woman he wanted.'

Arden didn't answer. Nan Clevenger had reappeared at the head of the stairs, carrying a carpetbag and a ridiculous hat trimmed with bright cloth flowers. Her face grim and determined, she handed Dulcie the hat and said, 'Now, let's go.' And she took a grip on her sister's arm, to turn her toward the stairs.

But suddenly Dulcie was screaming and crying, 'No! You can't make me!' She jerked to tear free of the grasp, striking at the other girl. Nan said something that sounded like a cuss word as she ducked the raking fingers. Next moment, Dulcie apparently got tangled in her skirts and tripped on the top step, and as she fell she screamed again—in fear, this time—and pulled her sister down with her.

Before anyone could have saved them, they were rolling in a tangle down the staircase, blue jeans and petticoats and the carpetbag Nan had managed somehow to keep hold of. Arden, leaping to catch them, was almost borne under. They reached the foot of the steps in a heap, Dulcie's screams mingling with a burst of wild laughter from one of Pete Hawks' painted women.

A movement seen from the tail of his eye warned Arden and he turned, then, just as Tab Slagoe whirled from his place at the counter with one hand streaking for his gun. Arden was not quite taken by surprise. He tipped the weapon in his hand and Slagoe was caught up short, as a bullet chewed into the floor between his boots. The explosion of the shot left its deafening echoes in numbed ears; it cut off Dulcie's sobbings and the happy laughter of the women. It left Slagoe staring at the dribble of smoke pouring from the black muzzle of the Colt in Arden's fist, and then the redhead opened his fingers and let his half-drawn weapon slide back into the leather.

'All right!' snapped Arden. He added, 'Maybe you'd better unbuckle it and throw it behind the counter. Same for you, Hawks!' They moved woodenly, but they obeyed. When the weapons and belts had thudded to the floor he still kept his own gun in his hand, judging it wisest not to give them any further temptation by holstering it.

Nan was already on her feet, looking a little dazed. She still had the carpetbag. Her wide-brimmed hat was hanging on her shoulders by its throatlatch; her hair had tumbled and there was a track of blood on one cheek. Knowing that Dulcie's nails had done that, Arden was not particularly gentle as he hooked a hand under the other girl's arm and set her on her feet.

Dulcie, he thought, was near hysteria. She tried to cling to him but he shook her loose. Her hat was a rumpled ruin of straw and cloth flowers; he let it lie. He said gruffly, 'Go with your sister, now, and don't make any more trouble. A dive like this is no place for you, and you know it!'

The older girl had quickly recovered. All brisk efficiency again, she grabbed Dulcie's arm and, before her sister could find the presence of mind to argue, was starting her for the door. Arden stood watch on Hawks and Slagoe until the screen door slapped shut behind them.

Pete Hawks' breathing was heavy in the renewed stillness. He said, 'Just remember what I told you! Frank Trace—'

'The hell with Frank Trace,' Arden grunted impatiently. Over by the kitchen, the cook stood gaping. He thought of the meal that was waiting for him and knew with regret it was one more meal he'd have to miss. He shrugged, and dropping his gun into holster he walked deliberately to the screen door and, pushing it open, looked back at the room.

Still no one moved. He stepped outside and across the porch. He didn't use the steps, but went over the rail and into the saddle of his waiting horse, whipping the reins free as he landed. Dulcie Clevenger was already on the back of the black her sister had brought from the roadhouse stable, her long skirt spread over the sidesaddle, one hand clutching the carpetbag; she looked a little rumpled, and her cheeks were shiny with weeping. On one of them Arden glimpsed a red mark and guessed that the flat of Nan's hand had helped get her onto the horse, and he thought grimly, *Good!*

All the nonsense seemed to have been knocked out of the younger girl, for the time being at least.

Nan was just settling into the saddle of her own mount, the blue jeans stretching tightly and making an attractive sight as she swung her leg across. No ladylike sidesaddle for her, he noticed with approval—an honest, rope-scarred stock rig, cinched to a roan that looked to have bottom and speed.

The freighter and his swamper, their teams hitched and ready to roll, stood beside their wagons and stared at these three people who had come hurrying out of the roadhouse in the wake of that single gunshot. Arden gave them no more than a glance. As he backed from the rail, he caught Nan's eyes studying him. She said quickly, 'You going our way?' and she waved toward the north, where Gunlock waited.

'I guess I am,' he said.

'Then I suggest you don't waste any time about it!'

He grinned at her, liking this girl. 'I suspect you might be right.'

'Well, let's go!'

She was already turning her horse and kicking it into a run. She had the reins of her sister's mount; Jim Arden put his buckskin alongside the other pair of horses and they spurted away.

In a matter of seconds they had crossed the clearing. The trees behind them made Pete Hawks' place fall from sight.

CHAPTER VI

Big Pete Hawks and the redhead, Slagoe, strode outside as the stranger and the two girls vanished from view. The moment the screen door slammed shut the slatternly pair of women were there to fill it, staring; but they knew their place—they didn't come any farther. Or perhaps they were afraid of the danger in Slagoe's angry, scarred face.

Hawks was eying the thinning fog of dust the departing horses had raised. Now, as the echoes of their hoofs faded among the timbered slopes and stillness settled, he turned to the redhead. 'That was him—that was Jim Arden! You gonna let him get away?'

'There's time enough,' Tab Slagoe answered. 'No place he can get to, in there! And right now I'm talking to *you*, Hawks. For the last time—what did you know about the Clevenger girl, and that note?'

The look the big man turned on him was curdled with fear. 'I told you! Nothin'. Nothin' at all!'

'And you really think Merl Riling's going to swallow that? Is he going to think Trace would have arranged for the girl to meet him here, without you being in on his plans?'

The roadhouse proprietor's dark face lost a little of its color. 'What—what do you figure to tell Riling?'

'What do you expect me to tell him? That it looks like Trace is fixing to walk out on him, cut his stick and run. And that you were hiding Dulcie Clevenger until he had a chance to send for her and take her with him.'

'It ain't true!'

'She was here, wasn't she? You had her hid upstairs, and you were trying to keep me from finding it out.'

'No, Tab! I—I just never thought to mention it. Never occurred to me Trace might be up to something Riling wouldn't like.'

The gunman sneered. 'I'll tell Riling you said so.'

Hawks made an anxious, clutching motion toward the other man. 'Do you have to tell him anything? Can't you sort of forget this? Hell, you know I never done you no dirt, Tab!'

But Slagoe was already turning away. A stringbean of a man carrying a heavy ax in one hand stood near a corner of the building, where he'd been drawn from his work at the chopping block. His name was Barnes, and like both Hawks and Slagoe, he was a Riling man. 'Where'd you put my bronc?' Slagoe asked him.

'In the shed. You want I should fetch him for you?'

'I'll do it,' Slagoe said, swinging down the broad slab steps. 'Saddle one for yourself. And get a gun. We're going after that Arden gent!'

Big Pete Hawks stood clutching the porch railing, watching the two of them head for the horse shed in back of the roadhouse. The sun that struck across him was warm, in a cloudless sky; but it wasn't warm enough to have caused the sweat that stood in beads upon his forehead.

Damn that Frank Trace! Thanks to him, Hawks was in bad trouble. He wiped a hand across his face; the hand was trembling.

*   *   *

When they had crossed the saddle of the pass, the trail tipped quickly downward; Jim Arden got glimpses, through a shifting pattern of timbered hills, of the green valley floor and an occasional glint of water. On its far side, to the north, rose a high rampart of hills capped with broken rimrock, which should make shelter for Gunlock Valley in winter. Though he wasn't a stockman, Arden recognized the signs of good range and once, as Nan Clevenger momentarily halted their mile-long plunge, he took the opportunity to say to her, 'Looks like a nice piece of cattle country you've got in here.'

She only nodded, briefly and distractedly. She seemed to have something else very much on her mind; now, looking around, she said, 'This way!' And she pointed left to where a spill of loose rubble had been left by some

47

ancient rockslide. She kicked her own horse out of the trail and into the rocks, towing Dulcie's horse with a sudden start that jerked the younger girl's head sharply and made her clutch for the saddle horn.

Jim Arden put his mount after theirs, glancing back once along the trail they were quitting before the shifting of trees and brush shut it away, and loose stones clattered under the hoofs of all three horses. No evidence of pursuit, as yet, from Pete Hawks; but he knew it would be coming.

Nan evidently knew these hills thoroughly. Observing the twisting course she led and the clever way she made use of terrain to blot their trail, Arden was willing to give over to her the problem of eluding pursuit; he didn't think he could have followed her tracks, with all his experience in man-hunting.

Finally, as though satisfied, the girl pulled rein in a little pine thicket. The horses blew and stomped and shook out their sweaty manes. The wash of wind in the sun-warmed pines mingled with a rippling of clear water from a moss-lined spring. Here she swung down, with easy grace, and tied her own and Dulcie's mounts to an aspen bole.

The younger girl had already slipped from her saddle and when Nan turned to speak to her, sullenly turned her back and stared up into the treetops, as though brooding over the wrongs that had been done her. Nan gave an angry sigh and a shrug, and didn't try to argue. She frowned and touched her cheek that was bleeding where her sister's nails had raked it. Jim Arden, dismounting, saw her wince. He pulled a handkerchief from his pocket and as Nan knelt beside the spring he offered it. 'This help any?' he asked; and when she looked up at him in surprise, he added, 'Go ahead—it's clean.'

She hesitated, then nodded her thanks and taking the cloth she dipped it and touched it to her cheek. At the sting of icy water she said to her sister, 'Darn you, anyway!'

Dulcie tossed her head rebelliously. The set of her pretty, spoiled mouth was completely unrepentant. 'I don't care! You deserved it. Because of you, I'll probably never see Frank again.'

'Just wish I could count on that,' Nan retorted as she dabbed at her cheek. 'Wish he *would* leave Gunlock and New Mexico and never bother us again!'

Dulcie whirled on her. 'Why do you hate him so?'

'I wouldn't think you'd have to ask. You know what he is.'

'I know what people like you *say* he is. I don't believe any of it.'

Nan looked up at the younger girl, and shook her head. 'Just how do you suppose he makes a living—he and those toughs he runs with? Why is he so thick with a crook like Merl

49

Riling, if he isn't one himself? Oh, Dulcie! If only you'd open your eyes and see past those good looks, and that charm he turns on when he hopes to get something with it!' She added, 'Had you stopped even once to ask yourself *why* he's pulling out, in all this hurry?'

'I suppose you know all about it!'

'I've heard rumors.'

Dulcie sniffed. 'Rumors!'

'All right, then! I got it from Dad, if you want to know!' Nan wrung out the wet handkerchief and spread it on a rock to dry. She settled back on her haunches, hands flat upon her thighs, and looked at her sister. In spite of herself, the other girl was waiting to hear what she would say.

'He told me Frank and Merl Riling had a terrible row yesterday. Riling was furious about some trouble Frank and the others got themselves into, down near Lordsburg. If Riling decides it's too risky to go on giving him protection—Well, I guess I'd run, too, if I were him!'

'It isn't so.' Dulcie cried. 'It isn't *so*.' Her cheeks were flushed, her eyes shining with angry tears. Then her glance settled on Jim Arden and she added, 'And why should we discuss our personal business in front of a stranger?'

Nan seemed almost to have forgotten him. She shot him a quick look; white teeth caught at her ripe lower lip. But as she swung to her feet, with a graceful economy of motion, her jaw was set firm. 'I'm not sure,' she said, 'that he hasn't made it his business, too, by what he did at Hawks' place. Tab Slagoe for one isn't going to let him forget it.'

'Just who is this Tab Slagoe?' Jim Arden asked, really curious to know. 'He dresses like a cowhand, but he doesn't look like one.'

'Everyone knows Merl Riling pays him gun wages,' she answered crisply. 'I hate to think of him giving you a bad time, just because you stepped in and helped me.'

Jim Arden hesitated. He could lie, but he supposed she'd be learning the truth about him in short order anyway. He said, 'Any trouble I have with Slagoe won't be on account of you.'

Her eyes frowned. They were gray eyes, he noticed; her hair, that she'd caught up now and pushed back beaneath the brim of her flat-topped hat, was taffy-colored and abundant, a shade lighter than her sister's. 'I don't understand.'

'Maybe I'd better tell you who I am. The name's Jim Arden. I'm a deputy United States marshal—'

As he'd expected, his words had a startling effect, especially on Dulcie Clevenger. The whites of her eyes showed as she stared at him. 'A *marshal*?' she cried. And then, in a voice freighted with suspicion, she said, 'And what are you doing here in Gunlock?'

51

'You've probably guessed. I'm looking for Frank Trace—for questioning in connection with that trouble your sister spoke about, at Lordsburg.'

Speech stumbled on the girl's lips; then she whirled angrily to her sister. 'There! I hope you're satisfied! You really filled his ears full!'

Nan was staring at the stranger, as though stunned. 'They'd send one man in here?' she exclaimed, incredulous. 'On a job like that?'

'The office is short of men. We spread as thin as we dare.'

She said, 'Well, now at least you know you're looking in the wrong place. Frank Trace has left Gunlock for good.'

'I'm not so sure. His plans may have changed, since yesterday. He got word somehow that I was closing on his trail and laid a trap for me, down at Sage—tried to get me murdered—'

'You're lying!' Dulcie broke in hotly. He went on patiently, not even looking at her.

'He probably thinks he succeeded.' Jim Arden thought of the bullet that had nearly tagged him last night, the voice that had called out, *'I got him!'* He went on. 'Trace may still be hunting that malpais for me. If he decides he succeeded in finishing me, he'll likely figure it's safe enough to come back to his stomping grounds and pick up where he left off. When he does show up, I aim to be right here, waiting.'

52

There was pure, malevolent dislike in the eyes of Dulcie Clevenger; he'd expected that. What really surprised and puzzled him was Nan's behavior. She was so openly hostile to Frank Trace, and all he stood for, that Arden would have thought she would look on himself almost as an ally. Instead, her eyes were cold and her manner suddenly withdrawn; her face looked pale beneath its healthy tan. She started to turn away, then remembered the handkerchief. Bending swiftly, she snatched it up and thrust it into his hand, saying, 'I'm through with this. You can have it back. Thanks.' And then abruptly, to her sister, 'Get in the saddle—you and I are heading home.'

The other girl shrugged and moved to her horse, without another word. Taking the reins of his own mount, Jim Arden watched them swing into saddles. He said, 'I take it there's some kind of a town up here?'

Nan looked down at him, and there was no trace of friendliness in her eyes. 'I'll show you the trail,' she said shortly.

'Thanks.'

They rode in a stiff and awkward silence, Nan leading and picking the way from her knowledge of the secret trails that webbed these slopes, Jim Arden bringing up the rear. Once or twice, as they crossed a bald hump of ground, he got a view of the valley—saw the flash of morning sun against running water, or glinting from distant squares of window glass.

Then they would drop into timber again, always riding slowly to spare their horses for whom these steep slants were hard going.

As he rode, Jim Arden's musings over the situation he had discovered here were increasingly interrupted by the demands of his empty belly. It was hard for a hungry man to concentrate on other matters, to the exclusion of his gnawing need for food.

At a sound of breaking branches, somewhere above them, Nan suddenly pulled rein. They were close beneath the overhang of a sheet of weathered rock, and they hauled up in its protection while Arden, rising in the stirrups, craned for a look up the hillside that was overgrown with scrub. Suddenly two horsemen broke into view and went quartering down the slant at a little distance from their hiding place. One was the redhead, Tab Slagoe; he carried a saddle gun in his hand and as he braced to the punishing downhill slant his glance probed the surrounding terrain, like a man on a hunt.

Jim Arden knew what he was hunting for; he waited tensely, one hand resting on the butt of his gun, until he was certain the man's questing search had missed the rock face behind which his quarry was hidden. Then, about to let the tension ease out of him, Arden cut a glance toward Dulcie Clevenger and was just in time to see her head lifting, her breast swelling to an indrawn breath. He didn't hesitate. He jabbed the buckskin with a knee and sent it leaping forward; its shoulder slammed into Dulcie's mount and both animals nearly went down in a tangle, in the treacherous footing. But it got him to the girl barely in time; he caught her around the waist and his hand clamped over her mouth, just as her lips opened for a shout.

Grimly he held her, as she fought him with her elbows and tried to free herself from the half-smothering hand on her face. She wasn't strong enough to break away, though she nearly pulled them both out of their saddles. Only when the Riling gunman and his companion were out of sight and he thought it was safe, did Jim Arden release the girl.

Immediately she turned in the saddle and was flailing at him with both fists, her face flushed with rage and tears blinding her. 'You filthy beast!' But Arden merely warded off the blows with an upraised arm until he had reined out of her reach.

'Maybe you'd like to be in the middle of a gunfight,' he said coldly. 'That's what you'd have started if they'd heard you!'

Nan Clevenger said, in weary disgust, 'Stop this, Dulcie.'

The younger girl subsided, but she scrubbed tears of frustration from her cheeks with the palms of her hands, leaving dirty streaks there. Nan swung her roan's bridles in a new direction, saying, 'Let's try this way. We're less apt to run into them again.'

Once more they rode. Half an hour later, at a place where a couple of narrow horse tracks split, Nan pulled in and pointed along one of them. 'We leave you here,' she said. 'That will take you to a wagon road that leads to town.'

Arden barely glanced at it. 'Thanks,' he said. 'But I've changed my mind. I think I'd better see you the rest of the way home.'

'That won't be necessary,' she objected quickly, her voice utterly without friendliness. 'Even Tab Slagoe wouldn't dare bother me again.'

'I should hope not,' he said. 'But that's not quite what I'm worried about. I just don't trust this sister of yours,' he went on, as Nan frowned at him in puzzlement. 'I want to be sure she doesn't get away from you. I expect to be seeing plenty of this Slagoe *hombre*, but I prefer to have it in town—not out here in the hills where a man can't watch his back.'

'Oh.' She seemed a little taken aback by his frankness, but after a moment she nodded. 'I suppose I can't blame you. Come along, then —if you're a mind to.'

'Thanks,' he said shortly, matching her mood. 'I would have, even without the invitation.'

She spurred her horse and Arden put his buckskin after her. Dulcie Clevenger rode between in hostile, rebellious silence.

Thus, Jim Arden made his entry to Gunlock Valley.

56

CHAPTER VII

The Clevenger place was a working ranch, a moderately profitable one to judge from the home spread. The log-and-fieldstone house had a solid look; the corrals, barns, bunkhouse and other buildings were in good repair. A windbreak of tall cottonwoods, with sunlight dancing on their leaves, let a snow of cotton drift across the neat patch of green lawn that fronted the deep veranda-fronted main building, behind its neat picket fence.

When Jim Arden and the girls halted, Dulcie immediately leaped down from her saddle, leaving the reins trailing. Without another glance at Arden, she flung open the gate and went running up the flagstoned pathway, across the porch, and slammed inside. He looked after her, with wry amusement tugging at the corners of his mouth. Then, catching Nan's eye, he said mildly, 'Thanks for your and your sister's company. If that's the road to town,' he added, pointing, 'I guess I can make it the rest of the way by myself.'

She nodded, and frowned. He almost thought she was on the verge of saying something, when a voice broke in on them from over near the corral. 'Judge! Hey, Judge! Looks like they're back. The girls are back!'

They both turned, still without dismounting, as the cowpuncher who had done the shouting was joined by a slim, silver-haired man who immediately started hurrying toward the house. Nan got down from her saddle and after a moment's hesitation Jim Arden followed suit.

This was, plainly, Nan's father. The family resemblance was beyond mistaking. He was, Jim Arden thought, a remarkably handsome man, erect and young looking despite the graying of his hair. Yet there was something about him—a troubled shadow in his eyes.

His voice was filled with alarm as he strode up. 'Nan!' he exclaimed. 'Where were you? I was about to send the crew out hunting!'

'It's a long story,' she said. 'It can wait. Dad, this is Mr. Arden.'

Clevenger turned to look at the stranger searchingly. He didn't offer his hand. 'Arden?' he repeated.

Jim Arden nodded. 'I believe I heard your man call you "Judge".'

The other made a deprecating gesture. 'It's honorary. I'm really only a justice of the peace. Anything I can do for you?'

'Well—' he began, and then Nan interrupted —too quickly, he thought.

'Mr. Arden is a federal marshal, Dad. He's here looking for Frank Trace.'

The surprise was plainly mirrored in the older man's eyes; but then his expression closed down and became cautiously noncommittal. The pause before he answered was brief but noticeable. 'I think we should go inside,' he suggested.

Jim Arden hesitated, then nodded. 'All right.'

They left their horses with knotted reins looped over the fence pickets. Clevenger opened the gate, and Nan preceded them in silence up the path.

The big door had a pane of frosted glass, worked with the design of a stag poised upon a knoll. To the left of the center hall, and the stairway to the second story, a tasseled archway led into a comfortably furnished living room; Jim Arden saw books and potted plants and a round center table holding a glass-domed oil lamp. There was a horsehair sofa, a couple of deep chairs cushioned in leather. On the mantel over the fieldstone fireplace there were pictures—photographs of Nan and Dulcie, and also one of a young man in his early twenties, who shared the good Clevenger features.

Dulcie herself had vanished into some other part of the big house. The three of them were alone in this cool, low-ceilinged room. Clevenger indicated a chair for his guest, but since Nan remained standing, so did Jim Arden, with his hat in his hands. The judge took a pipe from a rack on the mantel and proceeded to fill it out of a pouch of rough cut as he said, with what struck Arden as ill-concealed uneasiness, 'This business you have with Frank Trace—is it official?'

'Strictly. I take it you're acquainted with the man?'

'Oh, yes. We see quite a lot of Frank, here in the valley. He's well known in Gunlock.'

'Favorably, or otherwise?'

The older man's eyes met Arden's, then dropped quickly to the work his hands were doing. 'I'm not sure I know what you mean.'

'I can't believe that! This place may be isolated, but I'm sure you've heard rumors, at least, of the kind of thing he and his friends are charged with.'

'I've heard rumors. I've never seen any proof. You take a young fellow like that—a little wild, perhaps; all kinds of things tend to be laid at his door.'

'Uh huh.' It was the same line Trace had taken, in the dark of the barn last night. The judge might almost have been quoting him. 'Well, I'm trying to lay something there myself and nail it down with proof! Just to refresh your memory, two weeks ago, down near Lordsburg, an Army paymaster and his military escort—an officer and five enlisted men—were ambushed and murdered. Some fifty thousand dollars in cash was stolen. Does any of this ring a bell?'

Clevenger hesitated, then nodded. 'Of course, I'd heard. It was a terrible thing. But

60

are you telling me you can pin the blame on Frank Trace?'

'I'm trying hard. No case, as yet. As an officer of the law, it occurred to me you might be interested in helping to see justice done.'

The other took his time about answering. He had the pipe filled to please him. Now he took a match from a container on the mantel, struck it against one of the fireplace stones and busied himself with sucking flame into the bowl. His cheeks hollowed and smoke built a blue-brown cloud around him. Jim Arden glanced toward Nan. She stood by the center table, a hand resting on it. She was staring fixedly at her father, and Arden thought the hand was trembling.

Clevenger took the pipe from his mouth, flipped the burnt match into the fireplace and with a wave of his hand dispersed the tobacco smoke. He said brusquely, 'Just what day did you say this Lordsburg thing took place?'

'I don't think I said. But it was the twentieth.'

'Of last month?' The judge pursed his lips and shook his head. 'Then I'm afraid you're following a wrong lead, Mr. Arden. Frank Trace was in Gunlock on the twentieth.'

Jim Arden stared. 'Are you sure? I have a witness. I can place him in the vicinity of Lordsburg the day before!'

'I can only tell you the facts. Frank was here—here in my house. I know because it was a family affair. We were celebrating my son's twenty-first birthday.'

Arden suddenly felt a cold and unpleasant sensation in the pit of his stomach. He turned and looked at Nan, and saw what he could only describe as a kind of sickness reflected in her face. Yet when she found his eyes on her she met them with resolute determination.

He turned back to the judge. 'I suppose,' he said stiffly, 'you'd be willing to testify to this? In court?'

A shade of hesitation. 'Naturally,' Clevenger said then, and his glance was cold and level. 'So, Mr. Arden, it looks as though you've had your trouble for no purpose.'

Jim Arden passed a hand through his hair. 'It's kind of a jolt,' he agreed. 'It'll need some thought. Meanwhile, if you should happen to remember differently—'

'I'm sure I don't know what you mean,' the other retorted. 'What more can I tell you?'

He almost said, *You can tell me the truth.* But he knew that it would be no use. Suddenly he wanted out of that house, into cleaner air that was free of the taint of corruption. He said shortly, 'I won't take up more of your time.' He nodded to the girl, and he was already dragging on his hat as he walked out through the front hall and the big door with its pane of frosted glass.

Nearly at the gate, he heard her call his name. He turned reluctantly as she came

62

hurrying along the path. Her face was pale, her eyes troubled. 'You're going on to town?' When he nodded, she said, 'It may be dangerous!'

He dismissed the warning with a shrug. Instead he demanded bluntly, 'Why was he lying?'

Her attempt to pretend she didn't understand him fell slightly flat. 'What are you talking about?'

'I think you know! There isn't a word of truth in what he told me. He's willing to perjure himself—to alibi someone like Trace! It's bad enough, coming from any man; but a judge—an officer of the law—'

All color fled from her face. He saw her lips tremble; then her head lifted defiantly. 'You must be very sure of yourself, Mr. Arden. There's no power under the sun, I suppose, could make you falter one step from the path marked out for you by the oath you took and the badge you carry! I just wonder if you know what it is to be a human being!'

He stared at her coldly. He said finally, 'Perhaps I don't, since this isn't the first time I've been accused of it. Perhaps there's something left out of my make-up. But if it would let me see how any man could turn back on his sworn oath, I'd as soon do without it!'

'I thought I'd hear something like that,' she answered, and lifted slender shoulders. 'Very well, Mr. Arden. Let's see if you're as good as you must think yourself, to come in here and try to take Frank Trace singlehandedly, and pit yourself against Merl Riling's machine! As for my father—'

Even as she was speaking, the truth about the gray-haired man in the house struck him. It wasn't a pleasant truth, and it roughened his voice as he broke in. 'I think I already know about your father.'

There was a pause. She said in a small voice, 'You do?'

'It's this, isn't it: The local justice of the peace is a cog in that machine, himself—and I'm not particularly interested in knowing the reason why!'

That he'd guessed right, was plain from the stricken look she gave him. It left neither of them with anything more to say. Jim Arden, his own face grim, turned and shoved the gate open. He got the reins, lifted into the saddle of the buckskin.

Nan Clevenger still stood there by the fence, still unmoving, as he rode away.

CHAPTER VIII

The scene with the girl, and the angry sting of her words, rode more heavily on Jim Arden than he cared to admit. He'd got in the last blow, but he wasn't proud of it. He knew he'd never forget the look of Nan Clevenger's face as he'd left her standing by the gate, her anguished eyes holding the plea for her father that she was too proud to put into words.

Preoccupied with such thoughts, he almost ran into disaster. Only the rattle of hoofs crossing a stretch of hardpan, somewhere up ahead, reminded him he was in hostile territory. He pulled in sharply.

This wagon road was a dusty ribbon, looping its way through scattered boulders and stands of timber that prevented him from seeing very far, but that also gave a promise of cover. He cast about him, quickly settled on the nearest clump of cedar scrub, and kneed his buckskin out of the trail.

He had scarcely made the screen of branches, when a group of riders broke into view. There were three of them, traveling at a good clip. Arden saw the wink of sunlight on the guns in their holsters, and on the rifles filling the saddle scabbards. His eyes narrowed under the shadow of the hat brim as he watched them go by, leaving a mist of tawny dust in their wake.

He said, half aloud, 'Heading for Clevenger's.' Slagoe had got to his boss with the word, apparently, and they assumed Arden would be showing up there with the two girls.

He was loosening the hang of the gun in his holster as he came out of the trees and dropped into the road again, more attentive now. This was no time for daydreaming.

He sighted Gunlock without further interruption, as the road broke out of a band of timber and became the lower end of the town's single crooked street. He rode straight in. He figured the only thing was to keep pushing, keep his enemies off balance and try never to do what they expected of him.

It was an hour past noon, black pools of shadow beginning to lengthen as the sun slid over into the western part of the sky. Heat waves danced off roofs of tin and dry shingle, so that the whole upper half of the town seemed to waver like the lid of a heated stove. The street was quiet; a few horses sagged at hitching racks, and a mongrel dog dozing under the stoop of a barber shop lifted its head and beat its tail lazily a few times in the dust as he rode by, then flopped prone again. Down the street, a man left a building and crossed to the farther walk and clomped away down the dry plankings.

Jim Arden saw a sign: EATS. The word itself was enough to start his stomach juices churning, reminding him again of all the hours since his last meal. But as he stepped down into the hoof-pounded dust beside a hitch pole, he saw the smaller placard hanging from the knob of the door. CLOSED—SORRY. And he swore under his breath.

'You're no sorrier than I am!' he muttered. He knew the odds were heavy against finding more than one restaurant in a town this size.

Then, casting about, he sighted lettering on the glass of a saloon, directly opposite. FREE LUNCH WITH YOUR DRINKS. He knew what it would be—stale bread and dry cheese, and cold cuts beginning to curl at the edges; but he was in no position to quibble. He left his buckskin on the shadier side of the long street, and walked across. A last survey of the town, and then he pushed through the batwings and entered.

It was cavernous and dark inside, smelling of sawdust and sour whisky. Toward the back of the room a single oil lamp burned, putting a cone of light over a table where a couple of men were playing pool. The click of the balls ceased as Arden came in; the men straightened with cues in their hands and watched him as he walked over to the bar, skirting empty card tables.

Aside from the pool shooters, the only person in the room was the man behind the counter. Jim Arden told him, 'I'll take a beer.' The bartender didn't move for a moment.

67

Arden thought he was on the verge of saying something. But then he shot a look at the pair under the pool-table lamp, and he turned away reaching for a mug off the back bar.

Arden was already giving his attention to the free lunch, on a tray at the end of the bar. He was pleased to see the food was kept covered with a cloth, to discourage flies. Underneath he found the expected, and also some cold hard-boiled eggs in a bowl. He proceeded to build himself a sandwich, and then selected an egg and cracked the shell against the edge of the wood.

From the corner of his eye, all this time, he was watching the pair at the back of the room. To an observer he would appear not even to notice when one of them dropped his cue onto the table and, turning, clomped boots heels across the echoing floorboards and outside. Through a dusty window Arden saw him cutting at an angle across the street—a man on an errand.

Unhurriedly he ate his sandwich and egg, washing them down with beer, while the bartender puttered about and the remaining pool player leaned against the table and chalked a cue that didn't need it. The air was heavy with waiting and expectancy, but Arden pretended an indifference he didn't feel.

Something like this was what he more or less had counted on, when he braved setting foot in Gunlock town after all the warnings not to. He would play it out, see how they wanted the hand dealt. And, meanwhile, fill his stomach.

He was finishing a second sandwich when a mutter of gruff voices began to swell and boots struck the boardwalk outside the saloon. Jim Arden saw the bartender stiffen, heard him suck in his breath; and at the back of the room the pool player quickly laid aside his cue. Arden, casually turning, put both elbows on the edge of the bar behind him, as three newcomers shouldered in through the batwings.

Two of them were the biggest men Arden had ever seen. They were duplicates in size and build; moreover they had the same face, except that one was perhaps twenty-five years older than the other. Father and son, Arden quickly guessed. The older of the two had a deputy sheriff's badge pinned to a pocket of his unbuttoned waistcoat. Together they seemed enough to fill the room, and they dwarfed the man who'd come in behind them.

Arden had expected this would be the pool player who'd gone to fetch the law, but to his surprise he saw it wasn't. It was Tab Slagoe.

The gunman's face darkened with anger as he saw Arden again. The grizzled man with the deputy's badge gave him a questioning glance and got Slagoe's nod. He looked back at Arden then. He gave his sixgun belt a yank to settle it on slabby thighs, and he came forward with an odd rolling gait. His son followed a couple of paces behind, his stride matching the older man's exactly. They both halted, thumbs hooked identically into shell belts.

Small eyes in two wide-cheeked faces squinted at the stranger. The man with the star said, 'Your name Arden?'

'He knows it is.' Arden nodded at Tab Slagoe. He hadn't moved from his easy leaning against the bar.

'Then you're under arrest.'

Now, slowly, Arden straightened. 'Who says so?'

'This says so!' The big man tapped his metal badge with his thumb; his voice boomed and rolled through the empty room. 'I'm Luke Keefer. I represent the law in this here end of the county. My boy Ollie helps me when I need it. Am I going to need it with you?'

Arden looked up at the two flat faces. He was no small man himself, but they topped him by inches. He looked at the heavy shoulders and the deep chests of the two giants. He said, 'What's the charge?"

'Disturbing the peace. Assault with a deadly weapon and intent to kill. Those should do for a start.'

'You'll have to spell it out,' Arden retorted, his eyes narrowing.

'All right. You were up at Pete Hawks' place this morning. You started some trouble there. As a result, the place is a wreck; and when

Pete objected you pulled a gun and threatened to kill him.'

'This is ridiculous,' Arden snapped. 'And I think you know it. I wonder if you also know that I am an agent of the United States Marshal's—'

Tab Slagoe overrode and cut off those last words, saying quickly, 'Any talk you want to do, mister, you can do in custody. Take him along, Keefer.' And as he spoke his gun was in his hand, a deftly effective draw that put the muzzle squarely on Arden's middle. 'First get his gun. And take no chances—he's a demon with it!'

The bartender fumbled a whisky glass and dropped it, to smash on the duckboards with a startling sound. No one else moved. Arden stared at the gun that covered him. He hadn't known what they would try, but somehow he hadn't expected anything as gross and blunt as this. Chagrin flooded him at having walked into it.

At least one of the three thought he was contemplating some reckless action; with surprising quickness, Luke Keefer's giant son moved forward and his big hands fell on Arden's arm and shoulder. He tried to pull away but an iron grip tightened and next instant he was being spun around with effortless ease. He felt his arm jerked behind his back, shoved up between his shoulder blades with a force that shocked a cry of pain from him, and made his knees sag weakly. His chest struck the edge of the bar; a cold sweat started out all over him, at the thought that the man was going to pry the shoulder from its socket.

But the younger Keefer seemed aware of his strength. He merely plucked the gun from Arden's holster and then stepped back, releasing him. White of face, Arden clutched his shoulder as he whirled to face his captors again.

'That gives you an idea,' Luke Keefer said. 'Now, let's go. You can help him, Ollie,' he told his son. 'If he doesn't think he wants to.'

'It won't be necessary,' Arden said quickly, edging away. 'I'm with you!'

He had already spotted the jail—a squat log building, chinked with mud, with bars at its narrow windows. When they came out of the saloon and into the eye-squinting glare of sunshine again, Jim Arden turned in this direction; but at once a heavy hand pummeled his sore shoulder, pushing him around with such force that he nearly stumbled. 'That way,' big Luke Keefer ordered in his rumbling voice, and pointed him toward some place across the street.

Arden was puzzled as to where they meant to take him, but he wouldn't give them the satisfaction of asking; he supposed he'd find out soon enough. In silence they marched across the ruts left by iron-tired wagon wheels in wet weather, at which time the town would undoubtedly be a quagmire of mud hub-deep to a ranch wagon. They gained the farther walk. Another punch on his sore shoulder aimed the prisoner along this shaded side of the street; then abruptly he was halted at the foot of a flight of outside stairs, that angled up the side of a brick store building.

'Up there,' Keefer said.

There was no sign on the paint-blistered door at the top of the steps, or on any of the three doors opening off the dim hallway behind it. But at one of these, Tab Slagoe rapped with his knuckles and then turned the knob. Arden was ushered into a drab, dingy-looking room fitted out as an office, with a battered desk and file cabinet and a few stiff wooden chairs. There was no carpet, no curtains at the window that looked down upon the street—only the cheap green roller shade, cracked and battered.

If the room failed to impress, so—at first glance, at least—did the man who turned from a stand at the window. He was no more than medium height, a spare figure in a loosely-fitting sack suit and a collar that looked a size too large for him. He was probably not much more than forty, but thinning, almost colorless, hair accented the bony temples and sparsely-fleshed structure of his face. His color was bad. Thin, dry lips seemed to stretch with difficulty to cover a set of horsy, yellowish teeth.

But when the deep-set eyes turned on Arden, he caught something in their green depths that warned him: Here was a man to take seriously. He wasn't surprised when the redhead, Slagoe, said, 'Here he is, Mr. Riling.'

The boss of Gunlock surveyed the stranger with a single raking glance. He indicated a chair facing the desk. 'Sit down, Mr. Arden,' he said. 'We've got some things that need discussing . . .'

CHAPTER IX

For a long moment Jim Arden stood motionless, coldly regarding the other man. Behind him he heard the door close, shutting him away here with these four enemies. He said, 'I understood I was on the way to jail.'

'You are,' Merl Riling said. 'Don't get impatient.'

He came to the desk, seated himself behind it and piled his unhealthy-looking hands on the blotter in front of him. 'I told the boys to bring you here first. I want a look at you and I don't like it in that jail. It has a bad smell.' He lifted a yellow finger, then, pointing again to the waiting chair. The gesture was an order, though no words accompanied it.

Arden looked around. The two Keefers, father and son, stood glowering at him. Redheaded Tab Slagoe leaned a shoulder against the wall and with elaborate casualness cleaned the nails of one hand on those of the other. Arden shrugged, walked over to the chair and slacked into it, wincing at the throb of pain through his shoulder.

He pushed the hat back from his forehead and said, 'Of course, you know, you can't make this arrest stick. You've got no charge.'

'That's for me to say,' Riling told him crisply. 'Outside Gunlock, you may be a federal officer. Here, in my territory, that badge of yours is no more than a piece of metal.'

Arden shook his head. 'You've been running things to suit yourself,' he said coldly, 'until I'm afraid it's gone to your head. You may think you're bigger than the U.S. Marshal's Office, Riling. I promise you, you're not.'

'In Gunlock, I am!'

'No.' Jim Arden leaned forward, eyeing him directly across the desk that was scarred with cigarette burns, with the circular marks left by whisky glasses and the scoring of spurs. It would be hard to believe, if one didn't know, that this dingy office was the heart of an empire that controlled Gunlock Valley and reached its influence far beyond the circling hills. Call it a spider web, rather, with this grasping, yellow-skinned man seated at the center of it.

'You've got a nice setup,' Jim Arden admitted. 'But it can't last forever. Maybe local law is under your thumb, but that Lordsburg job was something else again!'

The bony hands twisted angrily together. 'I had nothing to do with Lordsburg. You can't pin it on me.'

'I think I can pin it on Frank Trace. And if I do, you're in trouble! You've been covering for him too long,' he went on, as malevolent anger glared at him out of the other pair of eyes. 'When it was only a few head of stolen cattle,

76

or the loot from some bank holdup, you pocketed your cut of what his gang brought in and there was nothing to worry about. But now that he's gone and murdered a federal man— your chickens are roosting, mister. This is one you can't get out from under!'

Driven by some roweling impulse, Merl Riling swung suddenly to his feet; the chair legs scraped worn linoleum. He took two strides to the window and stood looking down into the street, with both hands behind him and one slapping nervously into the other. The window was open. A few lazy sounds drifted in on the day's stillness, along with the scent of dust and sagebrush and a hint of pine-smell down from the rimming hills that Jim Arden could see, like black ramparts, far across the roofs of the town.

Merl Riling turned on his heel. He strode back to his chair, seated himself, and dropped both hands to the desk top in front of him. He leaned slightly forward and his eyes skewered the man across from him. 'How much do you want, Arden?' he demanded bluntly.

'I've got nothing to sell.'

Impatience rang in the man's harsh voice. 'At the right price, every man has something to sell.'

But Arden, returning the stare, merely shook his head. He saw a slow tide of color seep upward into the dry cheeks, turning them blotchy with anger. And over by the door, Tab

Slagoe suddenly shifted position and burst out, unable to contain his rage, 'Hell, boss! Don't let him bluff you. All it costs to get rid of him is the price of a sixgun shell.'

He meant it; Jim Arden felt the crawl of perspiration down his ribs, under his shirt, as he saw the same thought reflected in the look of those deep-set eyes across the desk from him. He took a slow breath and forced confidence into his voice—a confidence he was far from feeling.

'You're not a stupid man, Riling. I think you know you wouldn't have a prayer if you started murdering federal marshals.'

'If I do the job for him, mister,' Slagoe retorted, 'I guarantee it'll be done good. No body to trace, no proof that you ever actually came within miles of Gunlock. Just enough of a hint, maybe, so the next man they send will think twice before he tackles the job.'

'The next man they send will have an army with him.' But he knew from Riling's expressionless face that his arguments were falling short. Tab Slagoe laughed, openly.

'Don't try to scare us! The marshal's office hasn't got an army to spare. No, mister. You'll drop out of sight and that's the end of it.'

Merl Riling looked from his man to the prisoner, with his thoughts working inscrutably behind deep-set eyes. He sat back, then, scowling. He turned to the big man with the deputy sheriff's badge pinned to his greasy vest. 'We're getting nowhere. Take him along. Put him in the hole for a day or two. We'll see if that helps decide him to co-operate.'

Arden started an argument, then left it unvoiced. He saw Luke Keefer give his hulking bruiser of a son a nudge; and as the latter started forward, respect for the weight of that huge fist brought Arden to his feet before it could descend upon his aching shoulder. At a commanding jerk of the man's head, Arden turned and walked to the door and Tab Slagoe, sneering, opened it for him. The redhead said, with mocking cruelty, 'You're gonna love this, boy. The hole was just made for tough monkeys like you.'

He wouldn't allow himself to answer— either to offer further threats he couldn't back up, or appear to beg. He had a last look at Merl Riling's cold and expressionless face. Then he turned away and the door was shut behind him. Flanked by the Keefers, he found himself moving through the dark hallway and then out again upon the creaking flight of steps, into the blast of daylight.

The street was as empty as ever, yet he had a distinct feeling that many eyes were watching, behind nearly-closed doors and drawn shades. No one said anything during the time they traveled the half block to the jail, except once when they came to the place where Arden had left his buckskin gelding tied to the eat shack's hitch pole. He stopped and

79

said, 'What about my horse?'

'He'll be taken care of,' Luke Keefer told him, and again a shove from behind propelled him roughly forward. 'Keep walking.'

As they were approaching the squat, log-walled building, a couple of men stepped off the farther walk; they came a little distance into the street and Arden had the impression that they would have moved to intercept the Keefers and their prisoner had they dared; but then they halted, irresolutely. He wondered about them. They were still standing there, watching, as Arden ducked the low and crudely-hewn lintel, and disappeared inside.

The Keefers followed him in, and he heard the heavy door slam.

The jail office was small and not too well lighted by the windows, that were scarcely more than rifle slits behind their pattern of iron bars. Arden saw a roll-top desk with its pigeon holes stuffed with loose papers; a rack holding a rifle and two double-barreled shotguns; a rusty heater standing in its box of cinders.

Facing the street entrance was the jail cell. Apparently, there was only one. Its door was a thick slab of wood, reinforced with strap iron and riveted with heavy clamps. A tiny, grilled window at eye level showed sooty blackness. Looking at it and guessing what lay behind, Jim Arden felt his flesh begin to crawl.

Luke Keefer walked over to the desk and

laid Arden's captured six-shooter on it. He seated himself in a barrel chair that groaned under his weight, opened a ledger and took up a stub of pencil, which he rolled between thick lips to wet it. 'Empty your pockets,' he ordered.

Face impassive, Jim Arden handed over his wallet and his change, his knife and hip-pocket handkerchief, and watched them sealed into a grimy envelope and shoved into a desk drawer. 'You won't need the belt and holster, either,' the deputy said. 'I might as well keep all the stuff together.'

Luke Keefer laboriously entered the prisoner's name, the date, and the charge in his ledger. 'Put him in,' he told his son.

A massive padlock hung open on the door; Ollie Keefer lifted it off and swung the heavy panel back. Jim Arden took one step toward the opening, and halted.

The 'hole' had been rightly named.

He had never seen such a jail. There was no window, no light except what would come through the grill in the door planking. He saw, dimly, a double tier of bunks with what looked like rumpled blankets on them. An unbelievable stench compounded of sweat and stale food and urine hit him like a blow in the face, and he backed away from it.

He said, 'Forget it! You're not putting me in there.'

It meant a fight, as he well understood. He

saw the wolfish pleasure light Ollie Keefer's flat face as the big man realized he was meeting with defiance. The only chance was to get in the first blow. Arden stepped in under the massive hand that reached for him, and slammed a fist toward the man's jaw.

He missed; his knuckles struck a muscle-plated shoulder and bounced off it, with no effect whatever. He struck out with his other hand, futilely, in the same moment he tried to twist away from the reach of those other, clublike fists. He didn't quite make it; stars exploded around him as something took him on the side of the head with a force that slammed him half across the room, against a corner of the desk.

Pawing at the desk to keep his feet under him, he scrabbled through loose papers and suddenly felt cold metal under his fingers—his own gun, he realized, even as he got his hand around the butt and whirled bringing it up. But his arm was seized from behind, jerked above his head. Fighting to free it, Arden felt Luke Keefer's hot breath against the back of his neck. Almost with no effort at all the gun was plucked from his fingers and tossed aside.

Freed, he tried to get around to face both his enemies. A fist clubbed him between the shoulders and he fell like a log, toppling one of the barrel chairs as he went down.

He lay there, panting and drenched with sweat. The room seemed to wheel slowly around him. He'd lost his hat, and through a dangling screen of his own sweaty hair he peered up at his enemies. Father and son, they stood waiting and watching for his next move. They were only toying with him so far. Eventually, if he kept on, they'd lose their tempers; and then the fight would reach its inevitable end.

Ollie Keefer said now, "Want to play some more? Or are you ready to get in there like you were told?'

Arden didn't answer. He sat up, slowly. While they continued to observe his every painful movement, he ran a sleeve across his face, and then rolled to his knees and took hold of the chair, using it to help push him to his feet. He stood for a moment leaning over the chair, his hands on its arms. He knew he looked like a man out on his feet.

Ollie was the nearest of the two. When Arden straightened suddenly, whirling with the chair in his hands for a weapon, it was at Ollie that he made his lunge—all four legs of the chair driving straight at the man. Ollie stumbled wildly back, shouting in pain as a chair leg ripped along his cheek, tearing it open. He stumbled against the cold stove; braced there, he grabbed the chair and spun with it. Jim Arden was swung in a half circle and slammed hard against the logs with a jar that drove the wind out of his body. The chair was snatched from his grasp and flung aside;

then Ollie's hands were on him.

He was lifted off the floor. Ollie's bloody face, twisted now with rage and glistening with sweat, glared into his own. And then his head and whole upper body were being pounded, mercilessly, against the unyielding logs—twice, three times. He felt consciousness slipping, saw the world going black around him—black shot through with red, as his skull was slammed repeatedly against the wall.

He brought up a knee into the big man's middle and heard the gusting sound of pain break from him. The steel grip broke. Released, Jim Arden went to his knees and then forward on his face, hands stabbing out to break his fall. He tried to rise, couldn't. He raised his head and saw the door leading to the street; some blind instinct of will, that told him this was the way of escape, pulled him to hands and knees and started him crawling, weakly and painfully, toward it.

He brought up against something that broke his progress; stupidly, he looked at them—a pair of legs like tree trunks, in cracked and muddy jackboots. Painfully, then, lying there on his belly with his elbows against the floor to prop him, he looked higher, up the length of Luke Keefer's slabby shape. He saw the gleam of the metal star pinned to the front of the man's waistcoat.

Luke Keefer swore. 'You son of a bitch. Don't you never give up?'

A big hand came down, as Keefer leaned over him; fingers seized him by his hair and his head was jerked back until his neck seemed ready to snap. Piggish eyes glared down into his own. 'Son of a bitch!' the renegade lawman said, again. His other hand, fisted, drew back and then smashed full into the prisoner's face. He hit twice, and after that what light was left in the world faded and Jim Arden took the long drop into nothingness.

CHAPTER X

The voice, bodiless and impersonal, sank into Arden's muddled consciousness. 'You look like hell.' the man said. He knew the voice, but he couldn't put a face to it; then he realized why, and it prodded him the rest of the way to awareness.

It was a voice he had heard just once before—in the heavy darkness of a barn interior, without ever seeing the speaker's face at all. Blinking, he lifted his head off the sour-smelling pillow and looked up at the dimly visible shape of the man standing by the bunk.

All he could see was the outline of him, against the doorway. The door stood open, and dim daylight showed in the jail office beyond. Morning, he supposed. In the confusion of pain and numbed senses, Arden had been aware by fits and starts of a passage of hours; he remembered lamplight streaking in at him once as the door was opened and someone clomped in to set a tray of food on the stool by his bed. The food was still there, untouched. The night had somehow dragged itself out.

Frank Trace asked him gruffly, 'Can you get on your feet?'

'I don't know,' Jim Arden said.

He gingerly lowered a boot over the hard

bunk's edge and levered himself to a sitting position. He had to hold on to the framework for a long moment, or the ground might have rushed up and hit him in the face. He clung there while the room rocked and settled.

'God, it stinks in this place,' Frank Trace muttered. 'I don't see how anybody can stand it more than a couple of minutes. Let's go in yonder—air's better.'

A strong hand hooked Arden under the armpit and brought him to his feet. After that he managed by himself, steadier on his legs as soon as he was in motion. Carefully he walked ahead of the outlaw, almost stumbling once as an elbow struck the edge of the door. The dim light of the office hurt his eyes and he stood blinking a moment; then, turning, he got his first real look at Frank Trace.

He didn't know what he expected. What he saw was a man of nearly his own height, but a good half dozen pounds lighter—a slim, spare-fleshed young fellow, on a rangy frame that suggested a rather delicate bone structure within the denim jacket and jeans. Crisply curling, sandy hair broke beneath the brim of a pushed-back, sweat-stained hat, above long-lashed eyes set in an almost boyish-looking face, clean-shaven and with a mouth that seemed in repose on the verge of ready smiling. Looking at him, you had to remind yourself that there was evil in this man; for it didn't show.

Jim Arden could suddenly understand, for the first time, how a romantic young girl like Dulcie Clevenger could have lost her heart and refused to believe anything bad of him. The fact that Nan wasn't taken in spoke well for the older sister's solid judgment of what lay behind the smooth face and easy good looks.

The outlaw leader said, as a corner of his mouth quirked wryly, 'Well! So you didn't take my advice. I warned you.'

Arden nodded shortly. 'You warned me.'

'Either you're the biggest fool, or the bravest man I ever ran into. Maybe a combination of both. Maybe that's what it takes to make a man ram his head against a stone wall.' He added, 'How do you feel?'

'I've felt better.'

'You might look better, with some of that blood washed off your face.' A battered tin basin sat on a crude wooden bench in a corner of the room, with a water bucket on the floor underneath. Trace picked up the bucket and poured into the basin, and then stood aside. The water was tepid but it felt good against Arden's flesh, though it stung the cuts left by mauling fists. He splashed it generously over his head and face, and the water in the basin turned dully red as the dried blood soaked from his flesh.

Watching him, Frank Trace said, 'It must have been a real beating—an ordinary gent facing that pair of man-eaters! But I saw what you did to Ollie—and it was a hell of a lot more than I might have expected.'

As if to prove his words, at that moment the street door opened and Ollie Keefer himself strode into the office. He showed the marks of battle. His flat features were swollen and one cheek bore the ugly mark where a leg of the barrel chair had laid it open, narrowly missing his eye. He held up, staring at the open cell; then he turned and looked at the outlaw, and the prisoner rubbing his face dry against a sleeve. The giant loosed a roar.

'Hey! What's he doing out of the hole? Pa told me—'

Trace answered coolly. 'I want to talk to this man and I'm not going to do it in there.'

'But what if he—?'

The outlaw cut him short, imperiously gesturing the man to a chair on the other side of the room. 'Sit down and keep your eye on him, just to make sure he don't.'

Big Ollie looked like he might give further argument, but something in Trace's voice seemed to settle him. Glowering hatred at the prisoner, he slammed the door through which he had just entered, and walked over to the chair and dropped down on the edge of it. He sat there tensely, leaning forward; he'd hitched his filled holster around on the front of a slabby thigh and he kept his hand on the revolver.

'You better sit down too,' Trace told the

prisoner gruffly. 'Before you fall down. You still look like you're feeling pretty rocky.'

Jim Arden didn't deny it. He let himself painfully into the sheriff's chair, and Trace leaned a slim hip against a corner of the desk and stood looking at him coolly. 'I'd just like to know,' he said bluntly, 'what you really think you're trying to prove.'

'Nothing,' Jim Arden retorted. 'Except that no man is bigger than the law. That goes for you and Merl Riling.'

'You damn fool. You're only going to wind up dead.'

An angry impatience lifted Trace off the edge of the desk to pace the room while Jim Arden watched in silence and Ollie Keefer sat like a lump in his chair against the wall. The outlaw halted abruptly, facing Arden. He took a cheroot from his shirt pocket, bit off the end.

'I've got a piece of news,' he said, 'that you likely haven't heard, Arden. There was a fellow named McQueen—'

Jim Arden couldn't prevent the alarm from springing to his eyes as he heard the name; and he saw the other's lips spread into a look of amusement. 'I can see you know who I'm talking about,' Trace commented. 'The one who told you I was down near Lordsburg last month.'

'What about him?' Arden snapped; but he thought he could already guess.

'Why, I'm afraid he met with a little

90

accident yesterday. It sort of leaves you without a witness, Arden—without any way at all of connecting me with that paymaster job.' The outlaw let this soak in for a moment. His mouth hardened.

'Look, I told you, in that barn down in Sage I like your style; I don't like to see you throw yourself away. You don't know it, mister, but I've just been over in Riling's office—fighting for your life. He's about made up his mind that the thing to do with you is to take you out in the back country somewhere, plug you and cave a cut-bank in on top of you.'

Arden kept his face expressionless, concealing any sign of the cold thrill that pricked his spine. 'His man Slagoe was trying to convince Riling of that yesterday. Looks as though he put it over.'

'Tab Slagoe,' the outlaw repeated, and made a face. 'He wears his brain in his holster. All he knows to do when he finds a problem staring at him, is shoot it full of holes.'

Ollie Keefer spoke up, his heavy voice touched with a sneer. 'And what would *you* do with this star packer?'

'I'd give him credit for knowing a bad proposition, now that he's had a real look at it.'

Arden's eyes narrowed. He said coldly, 'You think I'm ready to quit?'

'For God's sake! What does it take to convince you? Another working over by our friend yonder? You wouldn't live through it.'

91

A snicker broke from Ollie's heavy lips, and the thick hands spread along his thighs flexed and worked as though in anticipation. And Frank Trace appeared to reach a decision. He said, 'Get on your feet!'

Jim Arden hesitated and then, a little apprehensive, came up from the chair. He was pleased to find that the nausea he'd wakened with had passed, and that the strength in his body was building again. Mostly he was aware of a gnawing in his belly. Honest hunger was a good sign, he supposed.

Puzzled, he waited to see what this man had in mind. Trace had laid his unlighted cigar on a corner of the desk; he looked now toward Ollie Keefer. 'Where's the stuff you took from him when you locked him up?'

Keefer scowled, then pointed. 'In the drawer. But—'

Not listening, Trace pulled out the drawer and found the envelope with Arden's name written on it. He ripped it open, dumping the contents in front of the prisoner, on the desk top. 'There you are,' he said. And Keefer came lumbering hastily to his feet.

'Hey!' the big man yelled. 'What do you think you're doing?'

Paying no attention, Trace was rummaging in the desk again; he came up with a gun and holster, shell belt wrapped around them. 'This yours?' He looked at Arden and the latter nodded. Trace drew the weapon from the leather, looked it over with professional approval. Then he rocked open the cylinder and calmly proceeded to kick out the shells, letting them patter one by one to the floor.

That done, he replaced the weapon and unwrapped the belt. As he did his eye caught the shine of the badge buckled to the underside. He lifted an eyebrow as he looked at it. Deliberate as an Indian husking maize, he stripped the loops with deft movements of his slim hands. When belt and gun were equally empty, he thrust them at the marshal. 'Take it,' he said.

Big Ollie Keefer could hold himself back no longer. He came charging across the room, a hand fumbling toward the gun in his own holster. But he held up, going motionless, at a single stabbing glance from the outlaw—a glance that flashed sudden danger. The big fellow dropped his hand quickly away from his holster, and he swallowed. 'You can't do this.'

'I'm setting up a practical demonstration for the marshal,' Trace said. 'I'm going to teach him a few important facts of life.' He turned to Jim Arden, who hadn't touched the proffered belt and gun. 'Take it!' he repeated sharply.

With a shrug, Arden took the belt, fastened it around his waist and settled it there while his puzzled glance tried to read the outlaw's face. 'The door's open,' Trace told him then. 'You're free to walk out of here.'

'Pa's gonna skin me alive!' Ollie Keefer groaned.

Jim Arden hadn't moved. 'I suppose,' he said coldly, 'you've got somebody waiting out there with a rifle.'

'Nothing as crude as that,' Trace said. 'I'm turning you loose, in order to show you just how hopeless this job is that you've taken on yourself. Of course, if you'd rather stay here—' He shrugged, his mouth quirking in a sardonic smile. Picking up his unlighted cheroot, then, he walked past Arden and through the door, leaving it open on bright morning sunlight.

Jim Arden stood scowling after him, wondering what kind of a trick the unpredictable man might be holding up his sleeve. But then a movement from Ollie Keefer drew his eye, and made up his mind for him. Left alone with the prisoner, Keefer was starting toward him, an evil intent plain in his face. Without further debating, Arden turned and walked out of there.

Coolness and the sweet pine scent of morning struck him. It was an incredible contrast to the foul, used air he had been breathing. Pulling in a deep lungful of it, he looked around quickly. There seemed to be no trap. Trace and a couple of other men stood by their horses at a hitch pole nearby. The outlaw was firing up his cigar; now he threw the match into the dirt and deftly swung to saddle. He reined in beside Arden.

94

'You're on your own,' he said. 'You really think you can bust this setup and turn the valley against us? All right, go ahead. Do your damnedest. But remember one thing. The trails are closed. There's no way you can get out of Gunlock, or send word out for help. It's you, all alone against me and Riling—the way you said you wanted it.' He picked up the reins. 'I've got a sporting proposition for you. I'll lay a bet that, before sundown, you'll be coming to me to admit you couldn't lick us with an army. You do, and I'll see you get safe conduct out of the valley. Wait till tomorrow, though,' he added, 'and far as I'm concerned you're fair game.'

Arden said coldly, 'You realize, of course, the minute you ride out of town the Keefers will be on top of me again. With only an empty gun, I'll be back in the hole—or someplace worse.'

The outlaw shook his head. 'I've taken care of that. Tom Daugherty's got his orders in case they should try anything—and they won't!' He nodded at one of the pair by the hitch rack. Arden recognized the tall, cadaverous shape and the piercing black stare of the man he'd seen checking the hotel register in Sage—one of those who had helped toll him into the trap at the barn. He leaned the point of a hip against the pole, arms folded, waiting and coolly competent.

The third man was mounting and kneeing

95

his horse toward Trace's, as the latter told Arden, 'So you've got a clear field, friend. Let's see how much good it does you.'

But at that moment Arden wasn't even looking at him. He was staring at the face of the rider who had ranged his mount alongside the outlaw's stirrup. Here was another face Arden recognized—not from life, but from a picture, from a photograph that sat on the mantel in the house of Judge Clevenger.

This good-looking young fellow, a member of the gang apparently, was the judge's son— Nan's brother! And as he watched the two of them ride off together through the early morning streaming of sunlight and shadow, Jim Arden felt he was only now beginning to understand some of the interplay of currents in which he found himself floundering.

CHAPTER XI

Hoof beats died, the dust settled in the street ruts. Somewhere a rooster sounded off in the stillness. Alone, Jim Arden looked around him, settling the empty gun and shell belt on his hips. Ollie Keefer stood in the jail door, glowering; but the big fellow made no move toward him.

Keefer knew the threat that Daugherty represented. Arden let out a small sigh of relief as he saw that the warning was respected. Daugherty was a dangerous man, and for the moment he had cause to be glad of it.

He would be happier when he was in a position to protect himself. And, seeing a general store some yards farther along the street, he turned and walked down there, moving stiffly with the many aches that plagued his battered body.

The storekeeper was sweeping dust out the door of his place of business. He stepped back and blinked at Arden, over half-moon lenses, as the latter entered. 'Morning,' he said, leaning on his broom. He seemed nervous and this was enough to tell Arden that the man knew who he was, and all about him.

'I'll take a box of .45 caliber shells,' Jim Arden said crisply. As the man continued to stare at him he added, beginning to anger, 'You carry them, don't you?'

'Shells?' The storekeeper swallowed. 'Yes, sir. I—'

'I'm in something of a hurry.'

The storekeeper retreated hastily before him as he strode into the room. Rounding the counter, the man was stooping to grope underneath it when a shadow fell across the open doorway. He glanced up, and Arden saw him stiffen. Slowly then he straightened and his hands were empty. 'Come to think of it,' he mumbled, 'I'm fresh out.'

Eyes hardening, Arden looked toward the door and saw Daugherty's gaunt shape leaning there. The gunman didn't need to say anything. Arden knew a blank wall when he saw one; and such a wall had been erected, in the blink of an eye, between himself and the frightened storekeeper. Argument was useless. He turned sharply and walked out, and Daugherty gave him a tilted, cold-eyed smile as he drew aside.

On the street again, Arden let a questing stare move along the street as he debated—aware, always, of the threat of Trace's man waiting silently nearby. Daugherty's job, he was beginning to see, was something more than that of a bodyguard.

For a moment he considered the windows of Merl Riling's dingy second-story office, almost ready to charge up there and have a showdown. But nothing would come of it, not with an empty gun in his holster.

Across the street, movement caught his eye. A green shade was just being run up behind the plate glass window of a building whose lettering proclaimed it the BANK OF GUNLOCK. As he watched, the door was opened from inside; a man in eye shade and black sateen sleeve protectors appeared in the doorway a moment, scanning the street, and then went inside again. The establishment seemed to have just opened for the day's business.

On an impulse, Jim Arden crossed the street and entered the bank's door. Glancing back, he saw that Daugherty seemed to be making no move to follow; perhaps he was satisfied there was no mischief to be gotten into here.

The bank was a small one, with a single teller's cage where the man in the eye shade was busying himself setting out a tray of coins and bills, getting squared away for work. Behind a railing, another man sat working at a desk; he was a portly, white-haired figure in a cutaway, a high celluloid collar and a severe-looking cravat with a stickpin. The banker himself, Jim Arden was willing to wager. Certainly, a responsible citizen if a town could boast any at all. He walked directly back there.

As he reached the railing, the man glanced up questioningly. Arden wasted no time on preliminaries. 'My name is Jim Arden. I'm a deputy federal marshal—'

That was as far as he got. The banker's face underwent a most alarming change; his cheeks went flaming red and then the color receded and left them oddly mottled. 'My God, Arden!' he cried. 'Why did you have to come here? Man, I—I can't talk to you.'

'Nobody can, apparently,' said Arden, and he felt anger begin to work in him, making his hands tremble until he had to clench them. 'What's the matter with this town, and this range? Is there nobody with the courage or self-respect to get up out of the dust?'

It was not the way to talk to a banker, but his feelings carried him away. He saw the other man begin to swell, head shaking until the jowls quivered. 'You don't understand!' he cried hoarsely. 'No outsider has a right to come in here and make reckless talk about a situation he knows nothing about.'

'I know plenty!' Arden retorted hotly. 'And I know that a range that lets itself lie under the heel of one man, or any group of men, is going to die eventually. Hell! You're a businessman, aren't you? Even if all you care about is a profit, and the amount of money in your vaults, I should think you'd care about trying to keep your town alive.'

The banker opened his mouth and closed it again. The soft and fleshy hands began to work, nervously, on the desk before him. 'You just don't understand.' he repeated. He would have made a good parrot.

It was no use talking to him at all.

Out on the street again, Arden began to get a sense of walls closing in. Suddenly he knew that it was strictly true, what Frank Trace had told him. He had a premonition that even if he went and knocked on every door along this street, he would meet the same answers, the same resistance, the same fear.

This town was cowed by the threat of Merl Riling's machine. Any man with self-respect must have left it long ago.

But, what of the rest of the basin? Surely, in a piece of country as broad as this one and potentially as rich, there must be a few with the gumption and the strength to stand up for their rights, especially if they were shown the way. Still, with the hawklike eyes of that lean gunman yonder checking his every move, he knew he stood small chance of getting away from this town, to find them.

Then he saw the eat shack sign and again was reminded of the growling of his empty stomach. But again the CLOSED sign showed behind the glass. Too late for breakfast this time, too early for dinner. So it looked like another trip to the bar lunch; cold meat and hard boiled eggs were better than nothing.

He walked along the splintered planking of the board walk, that rattled dryly under his boots; and across the way, Daugherty kept pace with him, confident enough, however, that when Arden pushed aside a panel of the swinging doors and entered the saloon, his nemesis let him go in alone, as he had done at the bank.

Arden was the only customer. The same bartender was on duty who had been there yesterday afternoon, and it looked like the same bread and cold cuts. As he watched, the man tapped the keg of beer for him, deftly collared the head of foam, and spun the glass across the wood toward him. As he did Arden glimpsed his own reflection in the bar mirror and was slightly shocked.

He needed a shave, and his face was discolored and swollen from the mauling the Keefers had given him. No wonder the storekeeper and the banker had looked startled, and the bartender had given him a long scrutiny before turning to draw his beer.

The man was watching him now as he set about gathering a sandwich together. And then, where he had least expected it, Jim Arden found the first glimmer of what he'd been looking for in vain. 'Mister!' the bartender said, speaking in a low voice though there was no one to overhear. 'How the hell'd you get out?'

'Frank Trace turned me out.'

'I heard tell that Riling ordered—'

'Trace countermanded the orders. But he emptied my gun first, and now he's making

102

sure I don't get out of sight!' Arden nodded toward the window.

The other man looked out and saw the ominous, bean-pole shape of the gunman. A passerby had stopped and the two seemed engaged in conversation, but Daugherty all too plainly had one eye cocked at the saloon entrance across the wide street.

'Look!' the bartender blurted suddenly; Arden, who had taken a bite of his sandwich, stopped chewing to glance at him. There was sweat on the man's bald head; one hand gripped the edge of the bar, white knuckled. 'Appears to me he's tied up for a minute or two. You really want to shake him?'

'I want nothing worse.'

'Take the alley door. I happen to know your horse was put in the stable at the end of the street. I can't give you more than a couple of minutes; then I got to yell for Daugherty or he'll know I done more than just turn my back.'

'Two minutes is fine,' Arden exclaimed. He added, frowning, 'If you think you can risk it. And why should you—when the town's merchants and even the banker himself haven't got the guts?'

The man shrugged. 'Maybe I ain't got as much at stake as them. I only work here.'

'You can bleed just as much, with a bullet in you. But, anyway—thanks! I'll take you up on it.'

103

'If you make it, you might look around. You'll find there's a few men that don't like what's going on and might even be willing to do something about it. Hunt up Sam Medara; he has a spread over west of the pass road. He can tell you who the others are.'

'Sam Medara,' Arden repeated, to set the name in his mind.

'I'd let you have a gun if I could.' The man's glance moved toward the window, and he gave a start. 'Hey! You better go if you're going. Looks like he might be starting this way.'

Arden stuffed the sandwich into his coat pocket, took a hasty swallow of beer to wash down as much as he'd eaten. Seconds later he was in the weedy wagon tracks that ran behind the buildings on this side of town, sprinting hard toward the livery stable that he could see looming above the other structures at the end of the street.

Two minutes he had, more or less. It had better be considerably more. He seemed on a treadmill, trying to force speed from legs that were still shaky. His goal appeared to be coming no closer, and at every step there was the expectation that Daugherty would come bursting out of the saloon and see him, and send a bullet winging after him. But the moments passed, and still he had the alley to himself. A cur dog, arrow-lean, came out from between two buildings and ran silently beside him, ominously sniffing his heels; it dropped out abruptly, without so much as a growl. And then the bare, unpainted wall of the stable was before him, and he found a door and slipped inside.

It was smaller than the one at Sage, five stalls on one side of a narrow aisle. There was the buckskin, and the saddle and bridle hanging on a peg. No sign of his saddle roll, but he hadn't expected to find it and didn't take time to look. The buckskin lifted its head in greeting.

At least someone had been feeding it, for the manger held the remains of a bail of hay and grain. Arden spoke to the horse, and whipped the blanket and saddle onto its back. He was cinching up when he heard the footsteps drawing near. At once he was at the door, waiting with his empty gun clubbed in his hand. Just outside, the footsteps suddenly halted; there was a moment of dead silence in which Arden, still breathing hard from his brief spurt of running, could only wait and try to muffle the pounding of his heart.

And then a boot ground on gravel; the door was seized and jerked open, the bottom edge hanging up as it scraped over uneven earth.

Arden's sweeping blow with the gun missed its target. The lath-lean shape of Daugherty lurched aside as the gunman turned, his own gun rising. Desperately Arden lunged straight into him, bulling him back against the rough edge of the door jamb, trying to keep that weapon from centering on him. His right arm came back and forward again, and this time he was lucky. He felt the butt of it strike solidly against bone, pass on and slam against the wall. The other man buckled at every joint. The gun flew from his hand, banging into an empty stall, and he folded onto his face in the ground litter of straw and filth.

Arden paused only long enough to fumble with the buckle of the outlaw's gunbelt; he jerked and the gunman rolled limply off it. The shells, in the belt loops, were .45's; so he didn't bother looking for the other gun. He flung the belt across the saddle, finished cinching.

Seconds later he was leading the horse out into the daylight, and already sending it into a hard lope before he was well settled in the saddle leather.

CHAPTER XII

After all the anxiety of trying to shake his bodyguard, the actual escape proved ridiculously simple. The livery was at the very end of the crooked street, and so far as he knew no one even saw him make his burst for freedom. A few long strides, and the buckskin had carried him into the first growths of brush and timber.

He pulled aside, beneath the sun-flecked shadow of a pine, and turned so that he could watch the town and the wagon road; as he waited to see if there would be pursuit, his hands were working quickly to strip shells out of the belt he'd taken from the gunman, and shove them into the cylinder of his own revolver. With the last chamber filled and the cylinder clicked into place, he felt suddenly a couple of feet taller.

Yet, it was disturbing, too, to realize how much he had come to depend on that gun—how much less a man he felt when he knew those five comforting bits of lead and brass were missing from their place at his hip. Sobered by the thought, Arden frowned as he held the familiar weight of the gun, his fingers curving naturally to fit the smooth shape of the metal and hard rubber butt plates. Then, shrugging, he shoved the weapon into his holster.

No sign of disturbance that he was able to see, yonder at the village; but he didn't know how hard a skull that fellow Daugherty might have had, or how soon someone might stumble on him and bring him around. Pursuit could be starting at any minute, and he was less than a fool if he waited for it to develop.

So, turning upslope toward the sheltering timber, he gave his horse the spur. He felt better when the wagon road was left below, and the straight red columns of the trees began to pull a shifting screen about him.

He was riding blind, having formed only the sketchiest idea of the layout of this valley. Somewhere west of the pass road, he understood, was the ranch of the man he wanted to see—Sam Medara; but even if he could find the place, he hesitated to do so until he was reasonably sure he wouldn't be followed. Accordingly, after some twenty minutes of riding he pulled up on a high point where he could see a long sweep of country, and any dangerous hint of movement behind him.

As he studied it, slacking his aching body to a more comfortable position in saddle, he worked at the captured gunbelt; he punched the grease-slick shells from the loops, transferred them to his own belt. That job finished, he tossed Daugherty's belt and holster into the brush. He took the reins, then, and was about to ride from there when something caught his attention.

A trail broke across a long slope, just below him; and now a single horseman had appeared, riding north along it at an easy canter. In the clear mountain air, the figure of the rider was quite visible though he couldn't make out the features under the flat hat brim. The slight shape looked decidedly familiar, however, and after a brief debate with himself Jim Arden made up his mind. Instead of turning back into the brush, he rode down at an angle that brought him quartering into the trail, ahead of the unsuspecting rider. He was sitting saddle, waiting with hands folded on the pommel, when Nan Clevenger suddenly broke into view across a hump of ground.

She pulled rein sharply as she discovered someone blocking the way. Then she saw his face, and astonishment broke across her eyes; her head lifted sharply. 'You!' she exclaimed.

'Morning,' Jim Arden said.

He didn't know what he expected, after the manner of their parting the day before. He thought she was staring at him oddly; for his own part, he was struck again by the extremely attractive figure she made, in a thoroughly practical hickory shirt and blue jeans and scuffed half-boots. He couldn't yet identify the expression that replaced the first, unexpected sight of him.

She said, frowning at him, 'I must have

heard wrong. They told me you'd been arrested, and had spent the night in that awful jail—in the hands of those terrible Keefers.'

'Your father's colleagues,' he reminded her dryly. It was a cruel thing to say and he was sorry as he saw it hit her. She stiffened; her mouth drew down. 'I shouldn't have bothered worrying about you,' she snapped. She picked up the reins and was starting to turn her horse when surprise jarred a question out of Jim Arden, and halted her.

'Wait a minute! Are you telling me you were heading for town only because you'd heard I was in trouble?'

'Well, goodness.' Her gray eyes wavered as though in confusion, and then she settled them squarely on his, with a slightly defiant jerk of her head; and he saw that color had been whipped into her cheeks. 'I haven't forgotten how you helped me yesterday. It's only right I should be a little concerned.'

'I should have thought that what happened yesterday had been pretty well washed out by this time,' he commented. 'Now that we know we're on opposite sides of the fence.'

She didn't try to answer that. She was looking at his face in a way that made him raise his hand and touch the back of it to beard stubble, and to a bruise that made him wince. 'What they told you was true enough,' he said.

'One of the Keefers did that to you?'

'Both of them! I raised a little fuss about

110

going into the hole. They had to persuade me. But, I went.'

She frowned as though in puzzlement. 'Then how did you get out? I understand—'

'You understood Merl Riling's orders were to leave me in there and let me rot,' he supplied. 'And I assure you, I'm grateful that the idea upset you. Maybe you'll be glad to know the orders were countermanded—by Frank Trace.'

Arden thought she gave a start. 'Trace! Is he back in Gunlock?'

He nodded. 'So perhaps you'd better be getting home, if you're still worried about your sister.'

'It isn't that,' Nan said, after the briefest of pauses. 'We're keeping an eye on her now; she won't get away from us that easily again. But, you'd better come with me. Those cuts on your face need tending, before they fester.'

'That's not too likely,' he began, about to turn down the offer. But then another thought stopped him. It would give him pleasure to be in the girl's company a little longer, strained though relations were between them. 'I could stand to clean up, though, and I could use a shave—and I lost my razor somewhere.' Again wiry beard scraped under his fingers.

Nan smiled suddenly, for the first time, and the effect was extremely pleasing. 'Then it's settled. You're coming with me'.

He put his horse alongside hers and they

turned back in the direction of the Clevenger ranch. But though they rode together, there was a distance of circumstances between them; the girl fell into a silence, and after a few tries at drawing her out, Arden gave up the effort. He knew she was troubled, and that his own presence here was a large part of it.

Ranch headquarters was silent as they rode in; the crew would be out on the range, and there was little sound except the wash of the wind through the cottonwoods about the house, and the voice of the ranch cook singing off key as he banged around the bunkhouse kitchen.

They dismounted and tied their horses at the gate and Nan led Jim Arden into the house and through it to the kitchen at the rear. She left him there, returning a moment later with a long-shanked razor in a case, a strop, a mirror, soap and a basin which she filled for him with steaming water from a coffeepot kept simmering on the back of the big cookstove.

'It's my father's,' she said, as she handed him the razor. He tried the edge on his thumb, and nodded approval. He promised his beard wouldn't damage it unduly, and set to work, standing at a window that gave him a view of the ranch yard, and of the range stretching beyond to the lift of timbered hills that encircled Gunlock.

When he had finished he looked almost presentable, despite the evidence of Ollie

Keefer's mauling fists. As he turned from the mirror, flattening the hair above his temples with the palms of his hands, he saw a look on Nan's face that he almost thought was one of approval. But she quickly altered this, frowning seriously instead. 'Won't you let me do something about those cuts?'

'They're all right,' he said bluntly. 'Honestly, they are.'

She retorted, 'You're a poor liar.' But she let it go, adding instead, 'How much have you had to eat?'

He had almost forgotten. With a rueful grin he admitted, 'Half a sandwich,' and fetched up the remainder from his jacket pocket—a thoroughly mashed and mangled handful of bread and sliced meat.

Nan made a face, and then she laughed as she took it from him and tossed it on the sideboard. 'Sit down,' she said firmly, pointing to the table with its oil cloth cover. 'I'll fix you something. And don't try to tell me you can't eat it.'

'Never!' he agreed, letting a grin break his dark and battered face. 'Now that I think of it, I've never been hungrier.'

It was pleasant to sit there, relaxed and at ease after the turmoil of the past thirty-six hours, and listen to the girl busy with the stove and the preparations of his breakfast. The odors of coffee and of frying eggs only helped to show him how hungry he really was. The

113

food, when she placed it before him, seemed better than any he had ever tasted; he told her so, gratefully.

She sat and watched him eat, in grave silence, refraining from asking the questions he knew lay heavily upon her. What did he plan next? What did he have in mind to do about her father? The questions were there, unspoken. And Arden became more conscious of the new, strained silence deepening between them.

He laid knife and fork across his plate, shoved them aside. 'Nan,' he said, and her eyes lifted to him. It was very necessary that he make himself clear. He took a deep breath, 'I hope you know there are things about this job I really don't like. I wouldn't want to hurt you; but—'

'But it's a job,' she finished, her tone oddly lifeless. 'And the job comes first with you.'

'It has to! Surely you can understand that when a man takes an oath—' He reached and took her hand, across the table; her fingers were cold, and they lay motionless and unresponding.

'I don't know,' she answered him. 'I'm not a man. I guess it's useless expecting me to understand how a man reasons.'

He would have tried again, but at that moment he became aware of arriving horsemen; from the sudden tightening of Nan Clevenger's fingers, he knew she was listening

114

to the same sound. It might be only some of the Clevenger riders coming in off the range, of course; but he needed to know. He came quickly to his feet, and walked through the silent house to the front door. As he halted there, looking out into the yard, Nan came up and joined him. He could almost feel the tightness in her as she saw the two men dismounting under the dappled shadow of the cottonwoods near where their own horses were tied.

Looking at the young fellow with Frank Trace, Arden said, 'What's your brother's name?'

He heard her gasp. 'How did you know he was—' But then she caught herself and answered, in a small voice, 'His name's Brent.'

'Seems to be pretty thick with our friend Trace,' Arden commented dryly. 'Was Brent at Lordsburg, along with Trace and the rest of them?'

'Of course not!' she retorted indignantly. But again conviction failed her and she could only add, 'I hope not—I hope and pray it! He's not a bad boy. But Frank Trace has got him under a spell, just like my sister Dulcie.'

'You seem to be the one member of the family that hasn't been taken in by him,' Jim Arden commented. And he stepped out upon the porch, as the two men came up the path from the gate.

They stopped dead at the sight of him. For a

moment there was no sound except the whisper of the wind in cottonwood branches overhead. It was young Brent Clevenger who blurted the question, as he stared at Arden, 'How'd you get here? Where's Tom Daugherty?'

Frank Trace told the boy calmly, 'Looks as though Daugherty may have fallen down on the job.'

'He fell, all right,' Arden said. 'Last I saw, he was flat on his face in the livery stable.'

'Dead?'

'Not unless he's got a softer skull than I give him credit for.'

Frowning, the outlaw ran a glance over the length of the man who faced him. Arden saw it touch on the gunbelt at his waist, saw the other's eye narrow and knew he'd caught the glint of brass studding the shell loops. Trace took a breath; his shoulders settled. 'I guess I underestimated you. Maybe Merl was right. Maybe—' In the middle of the word, he started the move toward his gun. Fast as he was, Arden's eye caught it. His own hand dropped to holster and he said sharply, *'Don't.'*

Trace's hand struck gun butt and his lean fingers wrapped around it; but the draw broke off there. The two men stood tensely confronted, motionless. And without taking his challenging stare from Frank Trace, Arden threw a warning from the side of his mouth at Brent Clevenger, whom he could glimpse

116

standing in an anguish of uncertainty at the edge of the scene. 'You too, Brent. Do you want a shooting right here in front of your sister?'

'Please,' Nan echoed, in a faint voice.

That broke the tension. Trace let the breath run out of him, and his hand dropped away from the gun. At once, Arden moved out of the slight crouch he had dropped into. Arms at his sides, he said, 'That's better.'

Brent Clevenger swore. Trace said heavily, 'And now what, Arden. Looks like a standoff.'

'Nothing's changed at all,' Arden said. 'Except I've had a little closer look at what I'm bucking. You and Riling have got a tighter hold here than I thought.'

'You still think you can crack it open?'

'You don't hear me yelling uncle.' Arden looked at Nan. 'My thanks again for everything, Miss Clevenger. I'll be riding.'

He turned and walked past the two men, toward the fence and his waiting horse. As he did he heard Brent Clevenger's harsh question, 'Frank, you gonna let him go?'

Arden half turned, waiting for a challenge. But Trace shook his head, and a half-smile warped his mouth. 'He won't get far if we don't want him to. I said I give you till sundown to admit you're licked, Arden. It still stands.'

Arden's only answer was a nod. He walked through the gate and mounted the buckskin.

From a little distance he glanced back once and saw the three of them under the trees before the house, still looking after him; he saw, too, a pair of riders coming slowly in off the bunch grass range, at an angle toward the ranch buildings; he saw the glint of Judge Clevenger's silver hair, the bright red of the scarf Dulcie wore.

He turned in the saddle and rode on, wondering what was the best trail he could take to get to the pass road and Sam Medara's, without crossing the path of danger.

CHAPTER XIII

In a dark mood, Frank Trace stood in the hallway of the big Clevenger house and watched the two girls mount the stairway. Just before the turn at the landing hid them, Dulcie glanced back and he saw the unhappy, despairing look she gave him; and he cursed under his breath.

Anyone could see what was happening. After that fiasco at Pete Hawks'—the note Dulcie had been stupid enough to leave where her family could find it—they were making damn sure that nothing like that happened again. Nan, the little bitch, was putting up such a guard that it didn't look as though there was any chance of his having so much as a word alone with Dulcie. After that business with Jim Arden, it was damn hard to stomach.

Scowling, he drew at the cheroot between his lips but it had gone out; he turned and walked into the adjoining living room, to get a sulfur match from the fireplace. Before striking it he stood a moment staring at the three smiling faces in the photographs that lined the mantel—Dulcie, Nan, and Brent. Suddenly, in savage bad humor, he flung match and cigar into the cold grate.

At the same moment voices reached him, muffled by the closed door that separated this

119

room from Judge Clevenger's office. The judge had taken Brent in there with him, after all too plainly turning Dulcie over to her sister's care. Frank Trace felt shut out, and this angered and alarmed him.

Was the judge really on the verge of rebellion? Was his hold on the Clevenger family beginning to slip away from him?

The rumble of voices came again. Quickly, Trace strode over and placed himself against the closed door, with an eye on the hallway to ward against anyone entering unexpectedly and catching him there. With his ear laid against the panel, he could hear every footstep, every movement, every word, carried through the sounding board of the door.

'I won't lecture to you.' It was the judge talking, in a voice heavy with emotion. 'It never did any good. Apparently you haven't cared that much about me, or your sisters, for it to make any difference. Then there's the Medara girl—a fine young person. I've hoped she might have some effect in curbing the wildness in you. I've hoped in vain.'

Brent Clevenger said, in a tone of anguish, 'Please, Pa! I know I've disappointed you.'

'You've done worse than that! You've made me swallow my pride and forget my oath of office! You've made me kowtow to a man like Merl Riling, and lie to a federal marshal to keep him from learning the truth about that mess at Lordsburg. And all because of

Frank Trace!'

'Frank treats me like a man,' the young fellow insisted stoutly. 'Instead of a kid, with my old man and a couple of big sisters breathing down my neck!'

'I know,' Judge Clevenger said heavily. 'Through the soundingboards of the door panel, Trace heard his footsteps and pictured him pacing in the narrow confines of the study. 'It's been my fault. I was so anxious to raise you in a way your mother would have been proud of, I did all the wrong things. But the question is—what do we do now? I've been thinking it over, and I can see only one answer.'

'And what's that?'

There was a long pause. The old man seemed pained by what he had to say next. 'You've got to leave Gunlock and New Mexico. Get out from under Frank Trace and Riling, before it's too late—even if it means I'm never to see you again.

'I was thinking perhaps San Francisco—or, you name the place. I'll pay your fare; and once you're safely there I'll forward a thousand dollars in cash. If I can afford it, I might be able to send more later. Well, what do you say?' he prompted when the boy didn't answer.

'I don't know,' Brent said in a muffled voice. 'It'd mean saying good-bye to Sue Medara. I could never ask her to come with me.'

121

'Well, you'd better think it over. And think hard. None of us are safe while that federal man is in the valley. I want you out of his reach.'

A chair scraped. Frank Trace took warning; quickly and silently he moved from the door, from the living room. He was on the porch, lighting up another cigar, when Brent Clevenger came out of the house with a black scowl on his youthful face. 'Well?' he demanded. 'What did the old boy want?'

Brent looked at him, through him. Without a word or a sign that he heard the question, he rushed down the steps to his waiting horse. He threw himself into the saddle and, jerking the reins, rode wildly away. He left Trace staring after him with narrow eyes, the cigar in his mouth forgotten.

He was jarred out of his thoughts by the voice of Nan Clevenger, in the door behind him. 'Frank! Where's Brent gone to?'

He gave her a cold look. 'I don't know,' he answered flatly; he made no attempt to use his personal charm on this girl, because she had made it plain long since that it had no effect on her. 'He never told me. Toward Medara's, would be my guess.'

Leaving her biting her lip in indecision, Frank Trace strode down the path and mounted his own horse. He made no attempt to follow Brent; he had other ideas. He took the town trail, that Jim Arden had ridden when he left the ranch a quarter hour before. And when he was out of sight of the ranch buildings he reined in briefly, pulled his gun and checked the loads.

Perhaps, he was thinking, his face bleak, he was wrong and Riling had been right all the time about this Jim Arden. His presence in the valley was already doing damage to what had been a nearly perfect setup. It had come between him and Dulcie Clevenger; and now, if it frightened the judge into sending his son away, it could end by destroying all his hold on old Clevenger and removing the alibi which was all that stood between him and a hangman's noose, for the killing at Lordsburg.

He clicked the cylinder into place, pouched the gun with a hard thrust. His mouth was grim as he took the reins and spurred ahead, wondering where he would be most likely to find Arden and settle this business once and for all.

*   *   *

Jim Arden had just dropped down the bank of a draw when he became aware of cattle being driven. He pulled up sharply, knowing any man he ran across could be an enemy; he was about to turn back and retreat into the brush he had left, when a better idea sent him spurring at an angle directly across the open throat of the draw while the noise of the approaching jag of beef grew constantly louder. He barely had time to spare; he went up into rocks and a thin screen of scrub, and there he pulled in and looked back and down.

Only yards from him, a dozen head of beef went by; he could hear the click of their horns, the pop of their ankles. The three riders who followed them at a slow walk, swinging yellow ropes, would have seen him had they bothered to lift their heads. But they went on, their attention lulled by the dull routine of range work. And Jim Arden rode ahead, after that, pleased to know that anyone who might attempt to follow his trail from Clevenger's would have little luck finding it again, now that those other hoofs had chopped it up.

It made it possible to take his mind off his back trail, and concentrate on what lay ahead.

Sometime later, at a fork in a wagon trail, he came upon a couple of crudely carved signs nailed to a slim-boled pine tree. One bore the name Medara and a Circle M brand burnt on with a running iron, and it pointed him in the direction he wanted. Sure now where he was, he gave the buckskin the spur in his impatience.

A single gunshot, somewhere dead ahead, warned him in time before he rode in on something too big to handle. Already he glimpsed the buildings of the ranch headquarters. At the sound of the shot he checked his mount quickly, and after a moment's debate he pulled wide and came circling in, to bring him in on the place indirectly and give him a look at whatever was happening, before he showed himself.

He thought he heard angry voices. A barn hid his view of the house and door yard; at the rear of the building he dismounted and dropped reins, and moved ahead along the side of it. And very suddenly stopped.

It was a more modest spread than Clevenger's; the house was board-and-batten, one-storied, and there were only a few outbuildings and a single, small corral. In the bare yard, a tense scene was being enacted. Three people, two women and a man, stood confronted by a group of riders—eight of them by Arden's count. He picked out the one who must be Sam Medara, and instantly recognized him. It was one of the pair of men who'd been in town yesterday and had watched him being marched into jail. They'd looked then as though they wanted to interfere, but couldn't quite brave the danger and the authority of the Keefers.

Now Medara stood clutching his right hand with his left, while blood dripped from his fingers in a startling crimson stream into the dust. His holster was empty; the gun he'd dared to draw lay on the ground in front of him. Tab Slagoe stood facing him, six-shooter smoking in his fist and big Ollie Keefer looming beside him.

The two women—they looked like mother and daughter—stood in the doorway of the house. They clung together in an attitude of sheer panic.

'It won't last forever.' Face twisted with pain, Sam Medara was shouting, hurling the words defiantly at Slagoe so that they carried through the stillness to where Arden stood unobserved at the corner of the barn. 'The writing's on the wall for you and Riling and your whole rotten machine. Now that a federal man's in the valley, you'll start seeing Gunlock people rise up. They'll put an end to you.'

Slagoe said something that didn't reach to Jim Arden. 'I ain't afraid of your guns,' Medara answered him, loudly. 'You don't dare do murder. Not even you!'

'Sam!' cried the woman Arden had pegged as the rancher's wife. 'Don't talk up to him. Don't egg him on.'

Whatever she read in Tab Slagoe's cruel face, the gunman made no move to use the smoking weapon again. Instead he looked at Ollie Keefer, and made a curt gesture with his head. Arden saw the big man nod, and then he was moving forward. Sam Medara fell back a step as Keefer prowled toward him.

The woman screamed once, shrilly. Then Keefer had reached Medara and his arcing fist struck with a sound like a hand slapping a side of beef. Medara was lifted and spun and dropped on his face in the dirt by the pile-

126

driving force of the blow. Arden, who had known the weight of that fist himself, winced as it landed.

Ollie Keefer, stooping, laid both hands on his victim and lifted him up, and holding him by the collar let him have a second blow and then a third, squarely in the face. He hit the man again and again. Medara's features turned as red as the hand and arm Slagoe's bullet shattered, and at last he hung limp in the giant's grasp. Keefer let him drop like a half-filled sack, and when he hit the dust finished him off with a couple of solid kicks of his heavy, cowhide boots. He stood looking down at the man, flexing his big fingers, not even breathing hard.

'That's a sample, mister,' Tab Slagoe said blandly, as Sam Medara stirred faintly and went still. 'If you got sense you won't ask for a second helping. You might not live through it!'

Without another look he turned and, holstering his gun, toed the stirrup.

Arden found his own gun was in his hand, the butt of it grinding into his fingers under the tightness of his grasp. He couldn't have fired at Keefer while the beating was going on, for fear of hitting the victim. Now there was no point in it. With the odds eight against one, he'd gain nothing by inviting a gunfight in which he couldn't win, and in which Sam Medara or his family could get worse hurt.

And apparently, Tab Slagoe was finished

127

here. In saddle, he waited until Ollie Keefer had mounted his own raw-boned horse. And then, at a signal from their leader, the group of horsemen turned their mounts and spurred out of the yard, and silence returned as the dust thinned and settled.

Jim Arden swore futilely, and shoved his gun into the holster. He turned to get his horse, and walked in toward the house leading it on the reins. The rancher was sitting up now, supported by his kneeling wife while the younger woman that Arden had taken to be their daughter hovered anxiously over him. It was she who heard the stranger's approach; she turned quickly and Arden got a glimpse of dark hair and frightened eyes in a young and wholesome face. Then the girl was whirling, snatching up the six-shooter that lay in the dust and turning it on him. 'Stay back!' she cried, and there was hysteria in her voice. 'Don't come near him again!'

Arden stopped in midstride. 'Easy,' he exclaimed sharply. 'I'm not one of them. My name's Arden. I'm the federal man they were talking about.'

She stared at him, the gun still leveled, and he wasn't even sure she'd heard what he said. But now Sam Medara spoke, in a voice blurred with pain. 'That's right, girl. He's the man I saw them throw in the hole yesterday.' Her father's voice must have jarred through to the girl. Her expression didn't change, but she slowly let the gun fall to her side.

'That's better,' said Arden. 'Now let's get him into the house.'

CHAPTER XIV

Sam Medara was not a big man, but there was an honest, sturdy quality about him that could measure up to more than mere inches in height or pounds of muscle. He was homely, rawboned; it was his wife who had brought what beauty there was into the family, and who had passed it on to their lovely daughter.

But the man who lay in the cheap iron bed seemed a different person from the fire-eater who had stood up to Tab Slagoe, not more than a few minutes ago. Ollie Keefer's mauling fists seemed to have taken something out of him. His face was as pale, under its blotching of freckles, as the pillowcase under his head, and the bandages his wife had applied to his torn flesh.

'They just rode up and called him outside,' she told Arden, her mouth trembling. 'I knew it would lead to trouble—the stand he always insisted on taking, against Riling and the machine. But, why this? Why today?'

'Because of me, I suppose,' Arden said heavily. 'Maybe they got it out of the bartender that he'd sent me here. Or maybe they're just making the rounds, passing the warning to anybody who might be inclined to listen to me.'

'There were some,' she admitted. 'Sam had

been working hard and I think he nearly had one or two talked to the point of backing him. I tried to make him be careful. I knew something dreadful like this was going to come of it.'

Arden looked at her for a long minute, reading the distress and the long worry that had tormented this woman. Sam Medara lay wide-eyed, looking at the ceiling as though he heard nothing. Arden turned and leaned over the bed. He found himself speaking in a louder voice, as though he were trying to reach the man through some barrier. 'Sam, you're not going to let this lick you? It's no time to call quits. The fight's just now out in the open! I carry a law badge, but I can't win the fight alone. I need the backing of you and the others.'

The eyes of the hurt man wavered, found his and held them for a long wordless moment. And then, still without speaking, Sam Medara simply rolled his head away until he was staring at the wall.

Slowly, Jim Arden straightened and his mouth was a hard, set line. The woman saw his face and her eyes blazed with anger. 'Well, what do you expect? What more can you ask of him? This happened because of you, you said. And haven't you done enough?'

'I guess I've done about all I'm going to!' he answered harshly, and he walked out of the house with a hard weight of futility riding him.

He went to his horse, lifted the stirrup fender and gave the cinch strap a tug that had all his grinding frustration behind it. Then, about to mount, he saw the girl standing by the door, solemnly regarding him. Some regret for his behavior inside the house caused him to walk over to her, leading his horse. 'Believe me, Miss Medara,' he said. 'I'm honestly sorry about your father. I hope he's going to be all right.'

She only looked at him, her eyes large upon his face. She didn't look like a person who would lift a gun against a man. She seemed a shy and quiet girl, now that the desperate excitement of their first encounter was past. A thought made him add, 'I suppose you're a friend of the Clevenger girls.'

Sue Medara nodded. 'I like Nan real well,' she said. 'Dulcie always struck me as kind of silly and stuck-up.'

'What about their brother? Maybe you can tell me, since nobody else will. How long's he been riding with Frank Trace?'

Somehow it never occurred to him he would get the reaction he did. Concern and fright darkened her eyes; she drew away from him while a hand rose to her throat. 'Brent isn't bad, Mr. Arden!' she cried. 'Honestly he isn't. One thing certain, I just don't believe he had any part in that Lordsburg killing. Oh, I *know* he didn't! He could never have hid the truth— not from *me*.'

132

So it was like that, was it? This girl was in love with Brent Clevenger; and naturally she would stand up for him, in the very same way Dulcie Clevenger insisted there could be no evil in Frank Trace himself just because she wanted to believe otherwise. But Brent Clevenger and the outlaw leader were different types; and so were the girls. Sue Medara was more like Nan. He detected solid character in her, and he didn't think she would be swept off her feet as easily as the flighty one of the Clevenger sisters.

Well, it didn't greatly matter. There wasn't much more, apparently, that he could do here or in Gunlock. The sense of frustration rose sourly in him again, and pulled him into saddle. He looked down at the girl but there seemed nothing to say. Instead, he merely touched his hat brim to her, and when he rode out of the yard, the buckskin leaped under the angry touch of the spurs.

There was no use trying to deny it. Merle Riling had him bested, at every turn. He'd been anticipated at Medara's; the smashing fists of Ollie Keefer had very definitely broken the one man he might have counted on. Now he was back where he started, with an added burden in the knowledge that his presence in the valley had been the cause of another man's beating and broken spirit.

When the news got around of what had happened to Sam Medara, no one needed to tell Jim Arden what the results would be. Any possible seeds of rebellion would be crushed. Medara's friends would be indignant and angry; but against the power of Merl Riling there was no reason to think they could be expected to act, once they saw what had been done to their leader.

Meanwhile the sun hung well down into the western half of the sky. He remembered Frank Trace's repeated boast that by sunset Arden would be coming to him to admit defeat, and ask for whatever terms the Riling machine felt like making. Could it be that Trace had called the turn, after all?

He felt the ache in his jaw muscles and realized his teeth were clenched hard. He reined in a moment, while he worked to settle his emotions. He was sitting like that, when a rider suddenly broke into view through the trees and brush ahead.

It was Brent Clevenger. They stared at each other, and then the young fellow drew a sudden sharp breath and began a fumbling motion toward the gun in his belt. He didn't make the draw, however; and next instant he was gaping into the barrel of the weapon Jim Arden slanted toward him, across the saddle pommel. 'If you live long enough,' Arden said coldly, 'you may learn the first lesson about guns. Once you start a play, you damn well better go through with it.'

The boy swallowed, and Arden could almost

smell the fear on him. He opened his mouth, but closed it again without speaking.

'This is the trail to Medara's,' the lawman said. 'On your way to see your girl, maybe? Takes more nerve than I'd have—after what was just done to her father!'

The other's head jerked. Words were jarred out of him. 'I don't know what—what you're talking about!'

'Slagoe and a half dozen others were there,' Arden told him bluntly. 'They sicked that animal Ollie Keefer on him—nearly killed the man with his fists. But a lot it should matter to *you*, I suppose,' he added, with a hard edge of scorn in his voice.

Shock broke across the boy's slack features as he heard the news. 'I didn't know!' he exclaimed. But then, reading the other's look, his expression hardened and turned stubborn. 'It's too bad—but he's been asking for it! Maybe it'll teach him a lesson.'

'You think so? Perhaps you're right,' Jim Arden agreed suddenly; it had come to him, just then, that there might still be a solution to his problem—that Riling himself had shown the way, and luck had put the tool in his hands. His mouth hardened. 'Let's go,' he said crisply, and waggled the barrel of the gun that covered Brent.

'Go where?'

'Just ride ahead of me.'

He had little stomach for the course he had

settled on, and he wanted to get it over with. In a brush-rimmed depression a few hundred yards off the trail, he ordered Brent Clevenger off his horse. As the boy stood watching with a look of puzzlement and apprehension, Jim Arden dismounted, walked over to him, lifted the gun from his prisoner's holster and tossed it away. Then, belting his own revolver, he suddenly and without warning struck Brent in the face, with all his strength.

Blood spurted from a split lip and Brent was sent reeling against his horse. He caught himself, barely managing to keep on his feet as he stared at the other. 'What—?'

'It worked for Riling,' Arden said, keeping his face and his voice empty of feeling. 'It should work for me.'

Seeing then what was in his mind, Brent tried to put up a defense, but Arden coolly knocked it aside. The boy was no match for him. Arden's punishing fists drove him back, licking murderously into his face, driving the wind from his chest. Suddenly he was down. Arden, standing over him, flexed bruised knuckles and said, 'You've got a choice. I can cut you to pieces like this—or you can give me what I need to know about the Lorsdburg killing!'

'Damn you!' the boy cried. He drove himself to his feet and lunged at his tormentor.

He was game. It touched Arden to see him trying to fight back; he forced down this emotion, willed his hard fists to continue their vicious and deadly work. But when a blow sent the youngster sprawling, bloodied and used, against the base of an aspen sapling, he still refused to stay down. With the breath painfully rasping through slack lips, he reached and grabbed at the trunk and hauled himself again, hand over hand, to his feet.

'Any time you want to stop, all you have to do is say the word.'

The boy glared at him through streaming hair and blood from a cut in his forehead. 'You want me to turn against my friends?'

'Do you honestly think Frank Trace would take this, on your account? For God's sake, kid—' He was very close to pleading.

And then there was a slam of pounding hoofs, and he turned as a shape hurtled toward him. He flung himself aside, barely in time; even so, the shoulder of the lunging horse struck him a glancing blow and nearly spun him off his feet. As he staggered and turned, Nan Clevenger was yanking the horse around and kicking it toward him again. She flung herself from the saddle and ran at him, her fists doubled and swinging. He took a blow that stung an eye big Ollie Keefer had blackened for him yesterday, before he managed to trap her wrists and hold her off him.

She'd lost her flat-topped hat; taffy-colored hair fallen around her shoulders, her round bosom rising and falling within the open-throated shirt, she glared into his face. 'You must be proud of yourself!' she sobbed. 'What are you doing to him?'

'I'm only doing what they did to Sam Medara, for daring to stand up for his rights.'

'But he's only a boy! I suppose that makes no difference, though.'

'If this will get me the evidence I need, I can't let it make any difference.'

She fought to pull free then, and he let her go. She stumbled back, brushing the hair from her face with an arm. Kneading her wrist, that his fingers had hurt, she glared as she said in icy contempt, 'I understand you now. You're not human. You're—you're a machine that happens to wear a law badge and a gun.'

Arden blinked, and for a moment he could do no more than stare at her, dumbly. They were words he had heard before, spoken by that other girl so long ago—words that had been written upon his soul in acid, so deeply that he had never been able to wash away the memory of them. And now, as Nan threw them at him, he tried to stammer a reply and could not, numbed as he was to hear them spoken again.

Suddenly Nan was crying, the way a little girl cries—unashamedly, her face twisted and lips trembling while her cheeks shone with tears. 'Go ahead! I can't stop you and I know he won't talk. Even if you kill him.'

He looked from her to her brother, who still stood clutching the tree and, with his forehead leaning against the bark, dragging deep, sobbing breaths. Suddenly, Arden knew what she had said was the stubborn truth. Young Brent might have his weaknesses, and his blind admiration for an unworthy idol. But he had Nan's strength, too; there was defiance still in the eyes that glared at him, sick with hurt and waiting dumbly for his punishment to continue.

A numbness went through Arden. He lifted his shoulders in a shrug. 'You win, kid,' he said heavily. 'You all win. I guess I'm not tough enough to play Ollie Keefer's game.'

They watched him, not understanding, as he walked to his horse, took up the trailing reins, and mounted. From the saddle, he looked again at Brent. 'But for your family's sake and your own,' he went on bleakly, 'you'd better get out of this mess before you're sucked under. Maybe you think Frank Trace is some sort of a god on wheels. You'll find out too late he's as much a rat as any other murdering renegade.'

Nan, her cheeks still flushed, was staring at him. She took a step toward him, and placed a hand on his stirrup. 'What will you do?' she demanded.

'Me?' He looked at her a long moment. 'I've got no choice, it appears. I'm going to have to go tell Trace that he's won.'

139

CHAPTER XV

He had ridden barely a mile when he heard a rider pounding up behind him. He pulled in, and a hand dropped to his gun butt as he saw it was Brent Clevenger, and saw the look on the boy's bloody face. But though he had recovered his own weapon, Brent made no move toward it. He drew rein and Arden said coldly, 'Well, what do you want?'

The boy colored under the lash of the words but he said, 'Was that on the level? You're quitting?'

'What is it to you?'

'Nothing, I guess. Except I at least ought to warn you—it's risky.'

Arden snorted. 'Thanks for telling me.'

Brent persisted doggedly, 'Slagoe, or the Keefers—if they see you they're likely not to wait for you to explain what you're after.'

'But not Frank Trace, of course? I suppose you'd have to see him shoot someone in the back before you'd admit he's capable of it.'

The boy's mouth tightened. 'I didn't chase after you to start an argument. I was gonna say, I'd be willing to ride along and make sure you got a chance to say your piece. If you wanted me to, that is.'

Arden could only stare. Slowly he nodded. 'I'd ride easier,' he admitted honestly, 'And thanks, kid.'

'No need.' Brent shrugged. 'You turned me loose when you didn't have to. I owe you this much, I guess.'

'You know where Trace would be?'

'Could be at Riling's ranch,' Brent said. 'But I guess the office in town. There was something said about a meeting there this afternoon.'

'A meeting? Interesting! The whole machine, maybe—including His Honor, Judge Clevenger?'

If he expected to sting an answer from the boy with that, he failed. So he took the reins and said, 'Town it is, then.'

Gunlock appeared quiet enough as the pair rode into it; it struck Arden that the life of the town must pulse at a very sluggish rate, even for so small a community. He wondered if the Riling machine helped to keep the vital fires banked low, giving it the lethargy he'd noticed each time he looked the place over.

They reached the building that housed Riling's office without incident, racked their horses, and were starting up the steps when the door at the top opened and the grizzled deputy, the elder of the two Keefers, stepped out upon the landing. When he saw Jim Arden he stared, gave a roar, and grabbed for his gun.

'No!' Brent Clevenger cried. 'It's all right. He came in with me—he wants to talk to Frank Trace.'

When Arden made no move toward his own weapon, Luke Keefer scowled but grudgingly he nodded and indicated they should mount the steps. As they climbed to where he waited, he snatched the marshal's gun from holster; with both gun muzzles trained on the prisoner, he seemed a little easier. He ordered Brent to open the door, and the pressure of a gun barrel was against Arden's back as they entered the building.

Young Clevenger opened the inner door and they walked into the dismal office. 'Look who showed up,' the deputy sheriff said heavily. 'Says he wants to talk.'

Arden's first glance showed that Judge Clevenger wasn't in the room. Did that mean the judge wasn't part of the machine's inner ring? As a matter of fact, there were only three men seated at the battered desk. Besides Riling himself, there was Tab Slagoe, and Frank Trace perched easily on a corner of the desk with a cigar glowing in his mouth. It was Trace who recovered first from his surprise. A smile tilted his lips. 'Well!' he said, around the cigar. 'Looks as though I win the bet.' He cocked a glance at the window, where a few streamers of glowing cloud showed above the false fronts across the street. 'Not quite sundown.'

The look on Merl Riling's yellow, bony face was one of complete incredulity. Looking at Arden he demanded suspiciously, 'You just rode in and let him take your gun? Is this a trick?'

'I'm all out of tricks,' Arden answered flatly. 'If there'd been a chance of getting at you with a gun, past your bodyguard, I might have tried it. But I know when I'm licked.'

'Maybe,' the boss of Gunlock grunted. 'If you don't—one more session in the hole ought to teach you!'

Brent Clevenger cried out, in indignation, 'Not the hole, Riling! That ain't fair. He didn't have to come in.'

This drew their attention to the boy, and Frank Trace demanded with a quick frown, 'What happened to your face, boy? What did you tangle with?'

Brent shrugged the question aside. 'That don't matter. I want to know what you intend doing with the marshal.'

'It's all right,' Jim Arden told the boy. 'Frank Trace and I made a sporting proposition.'

The lips pulled back from Riling's yellow teeth, in a mock smile. 'So I heard. Safe conduct out of the valley. You don't think you're going to get it?'

Arden had expected something like this from him. Instead of answering, he looked coolly at Trace; and he saw his look take effect, for Trace suddenly colored and swung erect, off the edge of the desk. 'He's right, Merl. It was a deal.'

143

'Now that I have my hands on him,' Riling said flatly, 'he don't leave Gunlock!'

'Frank! You gave your *word.*' Young Clevenger's exclamation held a sharp note of horror, and an appeal that Arden knew the outlaw couldn't afford to ignore. Trace, with an angry gesture, dropped his cigar into the spittoon beside the desk. 'Hell!' he said. 'Use your head, Riling. The man's admitting himself there's no way he can hurt us. With the judge's testimony there's no federal case against me. And that was the only excuse he ever had for attempting to mix in our local affairs.' He looked at Arden. 'You ready to ride?'

'Now?' The marshal shrugged. 'As ready as I'll ever be.'

'I'll take you as far as Pete Hawks'. You couldn't get past there without me.'

Merl Riling was on his feet, suddenly; he leaned across the desk with his spidery hands spread flat upon it, his eyes sparkling icy rage. 'Who is it gives the orders here?' he demanded. 'You or me?'

'In this case,' Frank Trace said flatly, 'me!' And he turned, in a sudden silence, to throw his challenging stare at Tab Slagoe and at Luke Keefer. They were staunch Riling men, but neither gave any sign of starting opposition. Trace let an edge of contempt touch his eyes; he walked directly to the grizzled deputy sheriff, who stood with a gun in each hand. He pointed at Arden's weapon, in Keefer's left fist. 'I'll take that,' he said quietly.

The big man looked at him, and at his boss. 'Hand it over,' Trace prompted sharply. Wordlessly, Keefer passed him the captured weapon and he shoved it behind his belt. 'We might as well get started,' he told Jim Arden. 'It will be dark in another hour or so.'

Merl Riling had slowly seated himself again, but his hands were still spread before him; his face was black with frustration and baffled rage, yet he too seemed no more ready to challenge Trace, than either of his henchmen. Brent Clevenger said, 'Frank, I'll just ride along with you.'

'No,' Trace answered. 'You get home and have someone take care of those cuts.'

'They're all right. I just think it would be a good idea for me to—'

'I said, get home!' There was a domineering note in Trace's voice, and a glint in his eye, that the boy couldn't argue with.

Arden had never heard him use that tone with the hero-worshipping youngster; he saw that Brent was taken aback by it. The boy's face blanched a little. His mouth sagged, and then he closed it and swallowed once, staring.

As for Jim Arden, as he turned to the door with Frank Trace close behind him, he remembered the glitter in Trace's eye and he could feel his veins run cold, with a first faint

145

premonition of just what he had let himself
into.

*   *   *

Daylight drained out of the sky; it turned to a
steely dullness that faded rapidly, and the
timber seemed to close in blackly on either
side of the trail. Eastward, the coming of the
moon was a promise and a broad flood of
silver glow behind the ridges. Then the moon
rose, and its glow paled the early stars.

The trail climbed rapidly now—the trail to
the pass, that Arden and the Clevenger girls
had followed in here only yesterday morning;
it seemed many times longer. He listened to
the horses' hoofs striking the dust, the creak
and pop of saddle leather and the snorting and
grunting of the animals. What little talk had
passed between him and the outlaw had
ceased in the first quarter hour after they left
the town behind them; now they rode in a
silence that was matched by the stillness of the
early night.

A hush lay on the darkening timber. Once a
bullbat swooped past them on flickering wings,
and later they watched a deer ghost across the
ribbon of trail ahead; neither one made any
sound at all.

Suddenly, Frank Trace said, 'Pull up,' and
his voice sounded startlingly loud though he
spoke quite softly.

146

'It's a long pull up to Hawks',' he went on, as they brought their mounts to a stand in the center of the trail. 'Maybe we can take care of our business right here.'

Arden felt the crawling in his belly. He said, 'What business have we got?'

'That depends.' The outlaw peered at him, in the moonlight that lay upon them almost like a physical weight. 'What happens after you leave the valley? What do you do about Gunlock?'

'You told Riling, yourself, how damn little there is I *can* do.'

He saw the other's head shake, under the shadow of the wide hat brim. 'I was talking for the kid's benefit. Brent knew I'd made a promise. He expected me to keep it.'

'I see. Then you don't really intend to?'

Trace lifted a hand, palm up. 'I keep my promises when I can. Sometimes it just isn't possible. You can see that, I guess. The kid is a problem. He gives me quite a time. It's no cinch, having somebody hero-worship you. It's a continual job trying to keep your hold on him.'

'Why can't you let him go? Why don't you take your hooks out of the boy?'

'Think a minute,' Trace retorted, 'and you'll see why I can't! There's the judge—'

'And Dulcie?' Arden added sharply.

He saw the man shrug. 'I'm not worried about her. She'll never turn. But, Clevenger has been working on his son, to try to get him the hell out of New Mexico and away from me. And if he manages—'

'Then, with the boy safe, he'll change his story and tell the truth and take away your only alibi for the Lordsburg job. And then you'll be fair game for me.'

He knew he'd read the outlaw's thoughts even before Trace nodded and said harshly, 'That's the reason I'm going to have to kill you.'

'It won't solve anything. There'll be others to follow me."

'Then I'll take care of them—one at a time. But you, damn it—you're the one who did it. You shamed the old bastard with your talk, and turned him against me. You blew everything to hell.'

With the last words, Frank Trace's calm manner broke and the wild fury inside suddenly broke through, lifting his voice into a shout. Arden heard the signal. He'd been waiting for it; as the gun suddenly rose from holster, shining in a blur of reflected moonlight, he was yanking the reins and spurring his horse straight towards the edge of the timber.

It looked like a solid black wall, but it opened to receive them. Arden scraped one leg savagely against the trunk of a tree. Behind him, the outlaw's gun exploded and the buckskin let out an almost human scream of

148

pain and terror; he judged that the bullet had creased it somewhere and drawn blood. Next moment, the horse had blundered into a thick patch of manzanita and as it struggled there, trying to free itself or to crash through, the gun roared again.

Arden, glancing wildly back, saw the flare of flame and it seared his vision so that for a moment immediately afterward he could see nothing at all but the smear of orange light printed on his retina. But the bullet had missed, that time. The buckskin had scrambled through the brush that held it up, and lurched forward as Arden blindly used the spurs, thinking only of putting something between him and that deadly weapon that was searching for him through the trees.

Back there, Frank Trace was shouting in insane fury, the gun smashing the night apart. Suddenly the horse under Arden smashed sideward into a dark pine, slamming its rider bodily against the trunk. His head struck the rough bark; stunning pain sheeted through him and numbed him. The strength went out of his body and he dimly knew he was falling, though his senses were so dulled he scarcely felt the impact when he hit the ground.

Lying there, fighting for the wind that had been knocked out of him, he heard the buckskin crashing away through the trees and brush without him. Out on the road, the firing had stopped; maybe Trace was reloading. But, no. Dimly, he was aware of voices, arguing. Who was out there quarreling with Trace? He realized then it was Brent Clevenger. The young fellow's voice, breaking hysterically, sounded very young against the outlaw's deeper tone.

There was the thin crack of another shot, and the talk abruptly ended. With an effort Arden rolled over and got a knee under him and then pushed dazedly to his feet, as the sound of a rider breaking into a fast canter came across the night; this faded and there was stillness except for the last dying echo of the hoof beats racketing off among the timbered ridges.

When Jim Arden made his way to the road, stumbling in the dark over windfalls and brush, dust was settling out like a faint silver mist. In the road a single horse stood on trailing reins; a body lay face down, unmoving. He went to one knee and turned young Clevenger over on his back, and saw the black wetness that could only be blood, beginning to drench the boy's shirt.

Brent's eyes opened, in a face that the moonlight gave a deathly pallor. 'Arden?' he muttered faintly. 'He—he didn't kill you?'

'It wasn't for not trying!' Arden said grimly.

'I got suspicious,' the boy said, speaking with painful effort. 'I began to wonder if he was lying and I had to be sure. I had to know if he was really everything I'd thought him to be.

150

So I followed. And I found out—'

He gasped as a spasm of agony went through him and twisted his face.

'Don't try to talk,' Arden said. 'Save your strength. I'll see how bad you're hit.'

'Where—where is he?'

Arden jerked his head toward the pass where the trail disappeared. 'He headed for Hawks'. He doesn't know I lost my horse, and he probably figures he's got to get there fast and plug the hole before I can escape from him. He'll be back looking for me, and he'll have Riling spread the alarm. Meanwhile, we've got a little time to see about getting you home.'

'I don't count,' the boy groaned. 'I've been a damned fool—believing, like you said, that Frank Trace was some kind of a god. Well, I know better now.'

'I said to quit talking,' Arden cut him off, sternly. And he began to rip away the shirt from above the raw bullet hole in the boy's body.

CHAPTER XVI

The wound was a clean one; the bullet had gone through without touching the lung, apparently. There was no sign of blood on the boy's lips, which would have been the tell-tale sign, and his pulse was strong. Arden plugged the two holes as best he could with their neck cloths, to stop the bleeding if that was possible. When he finished he saw that Brent had lost consciousness.

Fortunately the boy was light-framed, not too heavy. Arden got him into his arms, but after that it was no easy trick persuading Brent's horse to stand for him while he climbed, thus burdened, into the saddle. He made it, somehow; he distributed the limp weight as best he could, and turned the animal down-trail, back into the moon-filled valley.

He lost all sense of time; the horse lagged under its double burden, and Arden's body was a mass of aches and his arms numbed and devoid of feeling by the time he sighted the Clevenger place. He rode into the yard; the horse, knowing it was home, stopped and stood waiting but Jim Arden lacked the strength to dismount. The house and other buildings were dark. He raised a shout, and after what seemed an interminable time saw lamps being lighted. Judge Clevenger himself came stumping out of the house in his trousers and nightshirt, carrying a lamp in one hand, as a couple of members of the crew hurried over from the bunkhouse.

For long moments they all could do nothing but stare, until Arden said, half in anger, 'Take him, damn it! My arms are about to drop off. But, be careful—he's been shot.'

That shocked them into action. Hands reached and laid hold of the unconscious boy; gently he was lifted down and carried across the porch and into the house, and Arden was left, forgotten. Moving with an effort, he lifted his aching body out of the saddle.

When he touched the ground he had to clamp hold of the pommel and hold himself that way at first, to keep his knees from buckling. He almost groaned with the agony of the blood flowing again into cramped muscles. But after that he walked into the house, where he found Brent had been laid upon the living room sofa. It must have seemed too far to attempt carrying him to his bedroom on the second floor.

From the drained whiteness of his face, and his half-closed eyes, Arden couldn't even be sure he was alive. But apparently he was; for his sister Nan, in her nightgown and with a robe belted around her slim middle, was on her knees beside the couch, working efficiently and quickly to cleanse and bind the wound with antiseptic and clean cloths, while water in a basin on the floor turned red with the boy's blood. Dulcie and the two punchers stood watching, silent in shock.

As he saw Arden, the judge lifted angry eyes in a haggard face. 'By God,' he said, 'if you did this to him—'

Brent himself spoke, before the marshal could answer. 'No, Pa! It was Frank Trace.'

So he was alive, and conscious; his eyes held a feverish light and he would have tried to sit up but Nan held him back. In as few words as he could, Jim Arden told what had happened on the pass trail.

'Damn him!' the judge said hoarsely. His hands clenched.

'You were right about him, Pa,' the boy said. 'You and Nan—you were right all along. I'm ashamed that I thought he was anything more than a murdering snake. You got to help Mr. Arden put him where he belongs. You got to promise!'

Judge Clevenger's face looked sick in the light of the lamp on the table. 'Now, son—'

'I know what you're thinking,' Brent cried; beads of moisture stood out on his forehead, in the intensity of his effort. 'But it doesn't matter, not any more. I'm ready to take whatever medicine I got coming for the Lordsburg job!'

'Hush!' Nan said quickly. But it was no good. He went right on, despite her.

'I told you the truth about it. I swear I had

154

nothing to do with killing that paymaster, even if no court in the Territory would believe me. I guess I know now why Frank saw to it I stayed in camp that morning. He knew I wouldn't go along with a cold-blooded massacre. Just like he knew I'd believe him when he told me things had got out of hand and the killing was a necessity. Since I *did* believe him, there's nobody to blame but myself if I hang with the rest of them. But, Pa, it don't change what has to be done.'

The old judge looked at his son in anguish. Then, slowly, he nodded. He touched the boy's shoulder, and raised his eyes to the marshal. 'All right, Arden,' he said quietly. 'Whatever it is—name it and I'll back you, any way I can.'

'How many riders have you got that might be willing to use their guns?'

'There's half a dozen on the payroll, and I know you can count on them all once they learn what's happened to the boy.' Clevenger frowned. 'But it's not enough to go against Riling and Trace.'

'It can be if we catch them by surprise.'

'How? Trace will have sounded the alarm by this time.'

'All the more reason we're going to have to move fast. We'll try the town, first. If we don't find them there, we can try Riling's ranch headquarters.'

The judge lifted his shoulders and spread his hands. 'All right. I'm game. But if we run into the whole gang, we're going to wish we had some help.'

'We can *have* help!' Nan was on her feet, facing them both. She looked small and very feminine, with her taffy-colored hair hanging loose about the shoulders of her dressing gown; but she stood straight and determined. 'I'm willing to bet that if Sam Medara and the others only knew what was going on, they wouldn't hold back. I think they *should* know. In fact, I'm going to tell them!' She turned to Dulcie, who still stood as though in a state of shock, listening without seeming to comprehend anything that was being said. Nan laid a hand on her sister's arm. 'You stay with Brent. I'll get dressed and then I'll be riding.'

'No!' The judge had found his voice. 'Not alone, girl,' he protested. 'Not at this time of night.'

In the hall door she paused to give him a shake of the head and an indulgent smile. 'Honestly, Pa. When will you learn that I can take care of myself?'

Arden couldn't help smiling slightly. 'She's right, Clevenger. I've seen her in action—and she takes very good care of herself.' To the girl he added, 'If you do have any luck with them, have them join us in the timber just below the south edge of town. Tell them we'll hold back to give them time. We can use every man we can get.'

One of the punchers who had helped carry

156

Brent into the house said, 'I'll put a saddle on your horse for you, Miss Nan.' She thanked him and hurried off to her room. The judge stopped the man on the way to the front door.

'While you're at it,' he ordered, 'throw a tree on that bay gelding of mine and tell the boys we ride in half an hour.' As the man left with his orders, Clevenger turned again to Arden. 'You had anything to eat? I could use some coffee, myself—with maybe a shot of rum in it. No telling how long it might have to last us.'

'Sounds great,' Jim Arden agreed. He looked at the hurt boy, who was watching him out of eyes bright with pain. 'Take it easy, kid,' he said gruffly.

'You carried me down here from the pass, didn't you?' the boy murmured. 'What can I say?'

Arden shook his head. 'You've said plenty. If this thing works out tonight, there's just one person who's made it possible.'

*　　　*　　　*

In a town of mostly one-story shacks, the light that burned in Merl Riling's office window, halfway up the hill, gleamed almost like a signal. The riders pulled rein in the trees at the twisting street's lower end, and stared at the light in silence.

There had been no one to meet them, which

157

didn't surprise Arden. Even supposing Nan had any luck with the other ranchers, it was too soon to expect reinforcements. They would wait, and give them a chance to come.

Though the hour was late, Gunlock town showed lights in a good many windows along the dusty stretch of street. An oil lantern burned in front of the stable doorway, and another above the saloon entrance. But there was no movement on the street. A gusty wind had risen and it brought them an occasional burst of noise and the banging of a mechanical piano in the saloon.

'At any rate,' Clevenger muttered, 'I guess we found out what we wanted to know. Riling's in his office. He often works late.'

'Wherever he's at,' one of the riders said bleakly, 'you can bet he's got Slagoe or one or two of the others within call.'

They were silent again. Looking at the empty, light-splashed street, Jim Arden thoughtfully rubbed the back of a hand across his jaw. 'I don't know. There's something bothers me. You know, it could be a trick.'

'A trick?' Clevenger turned to frown at him in the filtered moonlight. 'You mean they might have guessed we were coming? It hardly seems likely.'

'I don't know about Riling, but Frank Trace isn't the kind to miss any bets. We can't afford to, either.' He picked up the reins. 'I'm going to take a closer look.'

The judge laid a hand quickly on his knee. 'You're not thinking of riding in there alone? Why, you're the one they want to kill. Let somebody else ease in and look around.'

'It's my job,' Arden said flatly, and kneed his borrowed horse forward.

The rising wind pushed and tugged at him, and drowned the night noises. When he reached the foot of the street, and the first of the town's buildings rose about him, he pulled over into the shadows as deep as he could. A keen sense of uneasiness rode in him, and he wasn't quite sure what warning was trying to make its impress. Something in all this seemed wrong.

A path of light from a window stretched across the moonlit dust; he skirted it carefully. A few doors below Riling's office he dismounted near a water trough that reflected the round white face of the moon. He tied his mount to the iron pipe, and laid a hand on the horse's shoulder as he scanned the street, seeing no movement. And while the horse dipped its muzzle and sent shivered fragments of reflected moon-disk scattering across the surface of the trough, Arden brought out the sixgun from its holster.

Like the horse, it was one he'd borrowed from Clevenger to replace the weapon lost when he was taken prisoner. He didn't like a strange gun; he frowned now as he hefted it, trying to familiarize his hand to the balance.

159

Afterward he moved up onto the sidewalk, and into the deep shadow of roof overhanging a building front.

He had no clear idea of what he intended, but he was sure of one thing. He wasn't going to have those other men follow him deeper into this, before he had settled his own uneasy doubts about a possible trap. It really began to look, though, as if he was mistaken. He'd come this far without any trouble.

Somewhere in the timber south of town, a sixgun cracked flatly.

He jerked around, alert in every nerve. A horse screamed. He heard a second shot, then three more in quick succession. After that the firing became general; and suddenly horsemen came breaking out of the trees.

The judge and his riders! Something had gone wrong down there.

Arden saw a couple of the men twist about in their saddles, striving ineffectually to return the fire that was pushing them out of the timber and into the open, forcing them up the hill toward the foot of the street where the houses began. As other guns that had been waiting in alleyways and on rooftops opened up on them, he knew in a single, blinding instant that his hunch had been right all along, and the whole thing was a trap.

CHAPTER XVII

Clevenger's men were hopelessly caught. Dust streaked the lantern light as they fought to control their terrified horses, with muzzle flashes spearing at them from a dozen directions. Arden saw a man spilled from his saddle and realized that he, himself, still stood motionless, as though rooted. That jarred him loose, however, and sent him running toward the place where he'd left his own mount.

He was groping for the reins when the animal suddenly gave a grunt and started to fold at the knees; Arden almost thought he heard the thud of the lead striking. Leaping back to avoid being pinned as the horse collapsed, he swiveled and fired at the flash of a sixgun atop a roof, across the way. His bullet missed; there'd been no target and the unfamiliar gun was a handicap. Then, directly in front of him, another horse screamed in fright and reared. Its rider lost his seat and went spilling to the ground, and Arden caught a glimpse of Judge Clevenger's silvered hair. Hardly thinking, he darted forward.

The judge seemed dazed, but not hurt. Arden got an arm around him and hauled him to his feet. At the same moment he caught sight of one who stood in the alleyway at a building corner, rifle raised to cheek. He thumbed off a shot, and was rewarded by seeing the man fling the gun away and crumple, lifeless.

'Take cover!' he shouted, into the racket of the guns.

No time to learn whether his voice had carried. Half dragging the judge's stunned weight, he managed somehow to get both of them back into the protection of the overhang. As they cleared the stiffening body of Arden's horse, a bullet slapped into the water trough and a tiny geyser broke and splashed them.

Clevenger groaned as Arden lowered him to the sidewalk planks. 'You going to be all right?' Arden demanded.

The old man waved the question aside impatiently. 'What about the rest of them?'

The confused milling, out in the center of the street, seemed to be ending. Horses were down; at least two Clevenger riders lay motionless. Arden knew that left not more than four in fighting condition. Whether or not they'd heard his shout, a moment ago, these had quit their saddles now to seek whatever cover they could find in the shadows along the building fronts; and there they were preparing to put up the best fight they could.

'It was a trap,' the judge said bitterly. 'Just as you predicted. They meant to catch us all out there in the street, and then seal up the ends and pick us off as they pleased. Only somebody must have lost his head and cut loose too soon.'

Arden scarcely heard him. He was listening to a rifle that was sounding off just above their heads. 'Somebody on the roof,' he muttered. As long as they stayed where they were, the shingled overhang would protect them. But Arden had other notions. 'Keep low,' he warned; then he was moving along the dark face of the building, and making a quick dive around the corner of it.

Back there was a lean-to, and a rain barrel set under the eaves. In a moment he had stepped up to the rim of the barrel and was lifting himself onto the lean-to roof. Dry shingles rattled as he slid over the edge; at once the rifle ceased. Then, as Arden came to his knees and lifted his head, he saw the rifleman silhouetted, waiting for him.

Arden ducked as the rifle barrel glinted moonlight. Muzzle flash seared his vision; the concussion of the shot struck solidly against his face. But the bullet passed him by a margin. He dropped his forearm, bracing it on the edge of the roof and triggered twice. The rifleman, in the act of jacking a new shell into his weapon's breech, cried out and was knocked over backward, in a grotesque sprawl.

Trembling a little at the closeness of that, Arden came up onto the flat roof and went forward at a crouch. The one he had killed lay atop his silent rifle. He snatched it up and turned to the low parapet overlooking

163

the street.

The firing continued, unbroken. From his new vantage point, Arden could see clearly three of the men posted along the roofs of buildings across the way. At once he went down to kneeling position, snapping the stock of the captured rifle to his cheek. Moonlight shimmered on the sights. He lined up one of these dimly seen shapes, and squeezed the trigger.

The rifle was a honey. As it slammed his shoulder he saw the man, yonder, double and plunge headfirst down the face of the building. Levering quickly, he swung the barrel and tried another target. He had to fire twice, but the ambusher dropped, knocked flat. This was more like it!

Something struck the low parapet in front of him; a splinter of wood, peeled free, ripped his cheek and drew blood in a streak of fire. He jerked around hastily. Perched on the comb of an adjoining rooftop, a Riling man had seen what was going on. As he fired a second time at Arden, the latter flung himself flat and triggered back. He heard a thin yell of agony. The man abruptly disappeared and Arden knew he had been sent tumbling down the far side of the roof's steep slant.

The rifle was growing hot in his hands. As he cleared the breech, turning to hunt more targets, he wondered how many more shells he had left. And where were the honest people of this town? Cowering in their homes, he supposed, lying low with doors locked and shades drawn—wanting no part of a fight they'd always shied away from. Or, maybe they didn't understand what was happening. Perhaps they figured it was the machine, fighting against itself, in which case, they would be as well off to keep their heads down, while both sides wiped each other out.

The swinging lantern illuminating the saloon sign opposite had just been smashed by a bullet. Burning oil spattered the building front and Arden saw the dry timbers catch in a number of places. The pungent smell reached him, laced with powder smoke and dust. With this wind behind it, a fire could grow and spread fast.

All at once, down at the foot of the street, the sporadic popping of guns seemed to have picked up tempo. Arden came to a stand as he tried to make out what was happening. He thought the guns that closed off the end of the street there were in some kind of trouble. There was a thin sound of yelling, a growing storm of hoofbeats. Suddenly Arden could see riders plunging through swirling dust, springing almost from nowhere. Now, what—?

He understood when he heard one voice shouting, 'Medara. *This way!*'

Already the front of the saloon opposite was a sheet of fire. Men came bursting out through the door, men who showed the beginning signs of panic. As they retreated before the withering heat, seemingly bewildered by it and by what had happened to their ambush, Arden saw a familiar shape—a rusty thatch of hair. There was barely time for a shot, but he whipped up the rifle and took it just as Tab Slagoe plunged across his sights. The redheaded gunman might almost have tripped over something, in midstride. He went down in a rolling sprawl, and Jim Arden knew that was one he could forget about.

Horses with emptied saddles came clattering by, raising the acrid dust. What had been a clear-cut situation, moments ago, was gone to hell now in a confusion of swirling action. But this rooftop perch was no longer a vantage point. Arden could see little now of what was happening—though what he did see was enough to tell him that Nan's mission must have been a success. The other Gunlock ranchers, under Sam Medara's lead, had come into the fight and as a result things had reversed themselves.

The Riling forces were taking the worst of it now. Unless he got down there quick, he might be too late for a part in the cleanup.

He left his post by the same route he'd come up, carrying the rifle by the balance. He made a leap from the lean-to roof, that jarred him briefly to his knees, and at the building's corner held up while he measured the situation. He didn't see Clevenger; the judge would have gone by now to join his men. Arden found himself very much alone.

Over the way, whipping winds had jumped the flames from the saloon to a store building adjoining; they made a pair of torches that flung sparks and flaming brands with a roar toward the high stars. They lit the whole street. And as he stood with cold air rushing in against his back, he saw—quite by chance— the one man he really wanted.

He nearly called out; but he knew Trace wouldn't have heard him above the crackling of the flames, and all that racket farther down the street. In another moment, the outlaw had vanished into the shadows and Arden frowned, wondering what he could be up to. Pulling out of the fight, perhaps? Leaving his men and Riling's to manage as best they could, with the odds gone suddenly against them?

Arden went pacing forward, intent on getting his man in sight again. The burning buildings threw his shadow, long and wavering, ahead of him: then it was swallowed up in dense darkness piled beneath the building arcades. He slowed, aware of a danger that Trace might know of his presence and be waiting to nail him as he came on. But even worse than this was the chance of the man getting away from him, and he went on despite the danger.

Then he paused, at a building corner, and there was the lighted window of Riling's office above and ahead of him. A figure was ghosting up the steps that crawled the building's moonlit wall. Before Arden could draw a bead, Frank Trace had already vanished through the door at the landing. But Arden was only seconds behind him.

When he eased into the hallway, he saw lamplight spilling through the door of Merl Riling's office. At that precise moment, a gunshot smashed deafeningly within the confines of the shabby room. In three strides, Arden reached the opening.

Powder smoke swirled about the shade of the desk lamp, and around the man who leaned over it. Cordite smell stung Arden's nostrils as he stood and watched Frank Trace pull out the drawer whose lock he had just blown open, and take from it a battered tin box. Trace put this on the desk top and lifted the lid, revealing the crisp green of new bills within. He nodded in satisfaction; as he closed the lid again his head lifted and he saw the man in the doorway, watching him.

Neither moved or spoke, during the long count of five. Then the outlaw said, 'Arden, damn you!' and the gun started to rise in his hand.

Arden slapped the butt of the rifle against his hip and his finger closed on the trigger. The guns mingled their explosions, and ear-punishing break of sound. Arden felt the red-hot, probing finger that dug deep into his thigh and brought him stumbling to his knees; but by then he had already got off his own shot from the rifle. There on the floor, he watched the heavy slug hurl Frank Trace backward, squarely into the window.

Glass went out with a smash, and the outlaw disappeared bodily, taking sash and shade with him. The look of surprised shock on Frank Trace was the last glimpse Arden had of him, before he dropped from sight through the opening.

CHAPTER XVIII

The skewered leg was so painful that he came crippling down the steps, leaning heavily on the handrail while his free hand grasped the rifle, with the tin box clamped under his arm. At the foot of the stairs he stopped to size up the state of affairs in Gunlock.

Apparently the shooting was over, and now the street was aswarm with people—townsmen, concerned chiefly with keeping the fire from spreading. Arden saw bucket lines forming and hurriedly passing filled containers from pumps and horse troughs, to wet down the roofs of adjoining buildings. He thought he saw the banker rushing about through the crowd, shouting instructions which no one seemed to heed.

The stiffening bodies of horses still lay where they had fallen; the downed riders appeared mostly to have been removed. But he saw one man who sat all alone on the edge of the board walk, rocking slowly back and forth and cradling a motionless shape in his arms. Arden limped over, leaning on the rifle.

The man was Luke Keefer; he lifted his head blindly and tears shone wetly, running down his grimy, rutted cheeks and into the stubble of gray beard. Looking at the figure in his arms, Arden saw the brutish features of big

Ollie Keefer. The giant's eyes were closed and his face was a bloody horror.

'They killed him,' the old man exclaimed, his voice trembling. 'They murdered my boy.' His shoulders shook with grief and his mouth pulled into a grotesque shape.

With no emotion at all, Jim Arden leaned and seized the deputy sheriff's badge on Keefer's chest and yanked it free. He said coldly, 'You're through in this town. You've got an hour to get out of it. Take him with you, for all I care. We'll get word to the county seat— ask the sheriff to send something better in the way of a deputy, next time.'

Keefer only nodded, dumbly, to show he'd heard. He was still rocking back and forth, moaning in grief, as Arden turned away.

Out in the street, another body lay in an ugly sprawl amid a wreckage of splintered glass and window frame. Arden didn't have to look closely to know he was dead; nor did he need the look on Judge Clevenger's blood-streaked face as the latter straightened from beside Frank Trace. The judge saw Arden, shook his head. 'Dead before he hit the ground,' he said roughly. 'Looks like a tunnel, blown right through him.'

Arden looked at the rifle in his hand, and tossed it aside; it was empty, anyway. He said, 'How many did we lose?'

'Three dead, that I know of. The doctor is patching up some bullet wounds now.' The older man looked closely at Arden. 'Man, I think you need him yourself.'

The marshal shook his head. 'Time enough for that. What about Riling?'

'Some of the boys cornered him in the stable, trying to throw a saddle on a horse. When he saw he was cut off, I guess he decided it was the end of the road for him. He put his six-shooter in his mouth and pulled the trigger.'

'Saved the Territory some expense and trouble,' Arden grunted. He indicated the box under his arm. 'This was Riling's share of the Lordsburg money. He raised a big fuss over it with Trace, but he didn't quibble about taking his cut! Trace was trying to get it for himself when I followed him into the office. So I guess that's the finish of the story. We'll probably never recover the rest; the army will have to be satisfied with this much.'

'Arden.' Clevenger's troubled tone brought his look to the man's face, visible in the light from the whipping flames. The judge ran a palm across his mouth; he looked very old and harried, in that moment. 'Brent told me he never took any of the payroll money and I believe him. He was really bothered about that killing; he wanted hard to believe what Trace had told him about it, but sooner or later I think it would have turned him against the whole dirty outfit. Do you suppose—' He lifted a hand toward Arden; then he let it drop again, with a hopeless shake of the head. 'But you'll do what you have to. Who am I, to ask a man like you for special treatment for him—just because Brent happens to be my son?'

Jim Arden looked at him a long moment, expressionlessly.

'Brent Clevenger?' he said then. 'Who the hell is that? I never heard of him.'

The old man stared, in slow-dawning understanding of what he meant. 'You're going to let him off? You don't intend to report—'

Arden cut him short. His head whipped around suddenly and he shouted in alarm, 'Nan! Stop your sister! Don't let her see this.'

He was too late. Dulcie had already caught sight of the man lying dead in the litter of the smashed window. She raised a hand to her mouth; but now Nan reacted to Arden's warning. Moving quickly she seized her sister's arm and tried to pull her back. Dulcie, whirling, struck at her; then the fight went out of her and suddenly she was in her sister's arms, her head on Nan's breast, while she sobbed with frantic and exhausted grief.

The judge said heavily, 'Well, I guess you know the rest now. You know why there was an ambush.'

'Dulcie?'

The older man nodded. 'She came straight to town, as soon as we'd left the ranch. She thought if she warned Trace, she could get him to go away with her before it was too late. But

173

she never dreamed they'd use her warning to lay a trap—or at least, that's what she claims.'

'I believe her,' Arden answered. 'She loved the man—thought she did, anyway. Well, she's young yet. She'll get over this.'

'I suppose so.' The judge straightened his shoulders. 'Right now she needs her father. And I've got to see about having the body cleared away from there.'

Arden stood and watched Clevenger go to join his girls. They talked a moment; then Dulcie turned from her sister and let the old man put an arm about her. Head down, blinded by grief, she let him lead her away from the stiffening corpse of the outlaw she had loved.

A sudden lassitude had settled over Jim Arden—a weariness born of too much tension, too many hours without sleep, and the draining of too much blood from the wound in his leg. He was looking for a place where he could sit when he heard Nan's voice beside him and felt her arm slip about his waist. 'This way,' she said; and not arguing, he let her lead him along the uneven planking of the walk. He found himself leaning heavily on her.

'Here,' the girl said. A packing case had been left in front of a store entrance; he sagged down on it, and put his shoulders against the rough boards.

He said, 'You saved the day for us, I guess. If you hadn't managed to bring the rest of them—'

'I was lucky. The leaders were all at Medara's having a council of war, so I only had to tell my story once. When they found out you'd talked sense into Pa, it was just a matter of sending for their crews.'

'I didn't show your father the light,' Arden corrected her. 'It was the boy.' And then he frowned, remembering. 'Dulcie left him there at the ranch. Hurt as he is, he shouldn't be alone.'

Nan smiled. 'Don't worry about him. He's not alone. Sue Medara headed for our place, as soon as she heard he'd been shot. I imagine she'll take better care of Brent than any doctor could.'

The girl came to her feet then. 'But *you* need a doctor, for that leg! I'll just go down the street, and—'

'No, wait! Please.' He didn't want her to go, even for that. There was something he needed to say, and he clutched her hand tightly as he tried to find the words.

But it was she who spoke hesitantly, while her warm hand returned the pressure of his fingers. 'Jim, I—I said something today that I'm ashamed of. I said you had a law badge for a heart—that nothing mattered to you but a record, and a job. It wasn't true. I know that now.'

'Maybe it was true, once,' he told her. 'But I've been taken down a peg or two. I've been

175

shown that it ain't always what it's cracked up to be—going it alone. Or maybe it's just that I don't want to go it alone any more.'

'Jim, you don't have to,' she murmured. She leaned, and swiftly kissed him. But when he reached for her she drew away. 'I'll hurry back.'

He sat there, amid the confusing sights and sounds of the firelit street, and listened to her move lightly away along the sidewalk planking.

We hope you have enjoyed this Large Print book. Other Chivers Press or Thorndike Press Large Print books are available at your library or directly from the publishers.

For more information about current and forthcoming titles, please call or write, without obligation, to:

Chivers Large Print
published by BBC Audiobooks Ltd
St James House, The Square
Lower Bristol Road
Bath BA2 3BH
UK
email: bbcaudiobooks@bbc.co.uk
www.bbcaudiobooks.co.uk

OR

Thorndike Press
295 Kennedy Memorial Drive
Waterville
Maine 04901
USA
www.gale.com/thorndike
www.gale.com/wheeler

All our Large Print titles are designed for easy reading, and all our books are made to last.